ONE OF
THE BOYS

ONE OF THE BOYS

DANIEL MAGARIEL

GRANTA

Granta Publications, 12 Addison Avenue, London W11 4QR

First published in Great Britain by Granta Books in 2017
Published by arrangement with Scribner, an imprint of
Simon and Schuster, Inc., New York

A CIP catalogue record for this book is available from the British
Library.

1 3 5 7 9 10 8 6 4 2

ISBN 978 1 78378 346 5 (hardback)
ISBN 978 1 84708 348 9 (ebook)

Offset by Avon DataSet Ltd, Bidford on Avon, B50 4JH

Printed and bound by CPI Group (UK) Ltd, Croydon, CR0 4YY

www.grantabooks.com

For my family

ONE OF THE BOYS

ONE

My father was swerving around cars, speeding, honk-ing. I rested my head on the strap of the seat belt, tried to ignore how fast he was driving, unsure if he was outrunning the storm or just angry with me. My mother and I had gotten into a fight. She'd called him to come pick me up from her apartment. He resented any dealings with her. It was midday, spring. A shadow crept across the fields. Crows looked on from power lines. The warning sirens wailed.

"Let me look at you," he said. He thumbed my earlobe. "Well?"

I looked to the road to remind him he was driving.

"What did she tell you?" I asked.

"You answer a question with a question? She said you were out of control."

"That's it?"

"Why is your face so red?" he said.

Embarrassed, I went quiet, kept to myself. He knew I'd

been crying. When we pulled into his driveway, I opened the door. He told me to shut it. I slammed it too hard.

"I was supposed to go to the movies," I said. "I'd made plans."

"Before the tornado watch?"

I nodded.

He repeated the question.

"Yes, before."

"Go on."

"I told her I was leaving, and she blocked the door, so I grabbed the phone and ran to my room."

"So today's the day she decides to start being a mother." He laughed wildly. "She had to hold you down?" he said, almost not a question. "Did she hurt you?"

I tried to remember. She had wrestled me to the bed. Then I was on my stomach. She twisted my fingers, took the phone. I tried throwing her off. That was when her hand holding the phone came down on my head. Now I fingered the tender spot on my skull, pressed it hard, wanting the pain, wishing the bump were visible.

"I don't know," I said. "No."

"Did she hit you?"

"I don't think she meant to."

He pulled me close, put his arms around me, patted my back to the rhythm of the wipers. It was an awkward hug. The kind of embrace you give to a grieving stranger.

"It's OK, son," he said. "It's OK." He sat me up. My older brother was standing in front of the Jeep, palms to the sky, shrugging at the rain just now quickening. "Let's go inside."

My father equated the granting of privacy with respect. Even when our bedroom doors were open, he knocked, waited to be invited in. We did not yet know why sometimes, when his door was closed, he did not answer. Since the separation he'd assigned each of us our own bathroom. His was still the master, upstairs, the same one he'd once shared with our mother. My brother's, the hallway bathroom, was on the same floor as our bedrooms. To decide who would get it our dad had measured the distance with footsteps—my brother's door was closer than mine. Two floors down next to the basement was my bathroom. Only on those late nights when, staring out my window, cigar tip aglow, my father would whisper me awake, *Be my eyes*, was I allowed to use the hallway bathroom, and only because he'd entered my bedroom without asking.

Here, in my bathroom, the Weather Channel spoke to us from the television in the basement. My brother looked at the Polaroids developing on the sink top. The ghostly shapes taking my form. My downcast eyes. My messy hair I'd made messier, shirt collar I had stretched to look rougher. My father seemed displeased.

3

"You look too good," he said. "You were in much worse shape when I picked you up, weren't you?"

It was a question meant to convince my brother.

"Yes," I said.

"Maybe more light?" my brother said.

He brought the lamp from the basement, plugged it in, tilted back the shade.

"Now, son, try to look how you felt when she hit you."

My father pressed the button. A photo reeled from the mouth of the camera. My brother placed it on the pile. We waited.

"Lamp help?" my father asked.

My brother shook his head.

"Fuck," my father said.

I held my breath, bit my lip until it bled, then took a bigger bite.

Two more photos.

"What do you think?" my father asked my brother. "What else can we try?"

"Makeup?" my brother suggested.

"You got any?" my father asked.

"Upstairs," I answered. "Next to his dolls and tampons."

"I could try slapping him?" my brother joked. "That might work."

My father turned to me. "How would you feel about that, son?"

My brother started to say something, that he'd been kidding, but my father silenced him. I'd hesitated too long.

"I thought you wanted to come with us," my father said to me.

"I do."

"I thought you were one of the boys."

"I am."

"Swear to me."

"I did already."

My father set down the camera.

"Why don't you make him swear," I said, pointing at my brother.

"Because you're the one who tells your mother everything," he said.

"Please, just do it," my brother said. "Just swear."

"You can stay in Kansas," my father said. He turned to walk out of the bathroom. "Your brother and I are leaving without you."

"No, Dad," my brother said.

"Fine," I said. "I swear. Again."

My father came back into the bathroom, picked up the camera. He put his hands on my shoulders, rotated me square with him.

"Close your eyes," he said.

I closed them.

"I want you to listen to me. Are you listening? When you were born, I mean right after the birth, your mother didn't want to hold you, either of you. She passed you off to me as soon as the doctor handed you over. I'd never seen anything like it. I mean, what kind of mother doesn't want to hold her baby? I can deal with the fact that she's never been much of a wife to me. But the terrible mother she's been to you? That has burned me for years. Don't you remember what I was like when you were young? Before the war?" *War* was the word he used for divorce. "I used to be a kid. We used to play together. The three of us. Remember?" Yes, I thought to myself, I remember. My brother and I are sitting on the carpet watching TV when suddenly we hear a low growl. We look at each other. There is no time to react. My heart quickens the instant before our dad on hands and knees crawls into the living room, roars. We climb all over him, working together to tackle the beast. "Do you remember, son?"

"Yes."

He squeezed my shoulders.

"This will end the war," he said. "No custody. No child support. This will get us free. Free to start our lives over. You'll see. In New Mexico I'll be a kid again. We'll all be kids again. How's that sound? Isn't that what you want?"

I nodded.

I heard my father load the camera.

My brother, I could feel, stepped toward me.

My eyes still closed, I locked my wrists behind my back. The beast is defeated, sprawled out on the carpet. My brother and I are lying on his stomach, facing each other. My brother's hair is darker than mine. Skin too. His coloring betrays a natural alliance with our father. They have the same sleepy, smiling eyes, which in sunlight turn brown as a bottle. I'm blond like our mother, with her hazel eyes. My ears, though, are my dad's, big like when he was my age. As the beast breathes, our heads rise and fall together, and with a smile he stole from our dad, which our dad probably stole from a movie, my brother's lips reveal his top row of teeth like a slow-rising curtain. I opened my eyes. My brother's arm was drawn back, ready to swing. I did not want him to hit me. I did not want him to have to hit me.

"Wait," I said.

"What?" my father said.

In the mirror I remade my face with sorrow. This will get us free, I told myself. This was what they needed from me. With my right hand I slapped my right cheek. The left cheek with my left hand, then again, harder, alternating sides, following through a little further each time so that eventually my head turned not from the flinch but from the blow. With my right, with my left, with my right, with my left. I faced my father. "Now,"

I said. "Take it now." I showed him my cheek. "This angle." With my right, my right, my right. "Again," I said. "Another. Take another."

My brother pulled each photo from the mouth of the camera. My father kept clicking until the button stuck. After they developed, we chose five of the Polaroids to show Child Protective Services.

An hour later, rain streaming down the one window, the basement had grown dark. The three of us quietly watched the weather report. The storm, which at first had looked like an amoeba shifting across the screen, had become unmoving bands of red and orange, as if the television had frozen, or the storm had turned sedentary, a new land formation across eastern Kansas. My father was hunched over in his chair, the heels of his shoes clamped to the bottom rung. He was about to spring.

"Let's go hunt twisters," he said.

We drove to the water tower.

Darkness advanced, not from the east, but the west. From the clouds at the front of the storm there was lightning. An enormous flock of birds warped in the wind. My father offered a reward to whoever spotted the first tornado. We stayed there for some time, our eyes peeled, closely surveying the horizon. But we saw none and eventually drove off. At home our fence had been torn from the ground. When my father saw the damage, he laughed and said, "Looks like the storm was hunting us," and after we moved to New Mexico, he referenced this whenever something worked out, and also whenever something did not.

TWO

My brother and I were in the park behind our new apartment, chasing lizards from the shrubs. We'd sold the house in Kansas, moved to Albuquerque. The three of us had driven out in the Jeep. My father had done the sixteen hours straight, except for a stretch in Oklahoma when my brother took over. My brother was starting high school in a few weeks, so our dad had figured it was a good time for him to learn how to drive on a highway. Though I was only going to be a seventh grader, I'd already begun to study how my father worked the clutch. I'd surprise him whenever he decided it was my time to learn.

The moving truck had arrived the day after us, and my brother and I had unpacked our father's bedroom before our own—the first room we'd ever shared. I'd also done the kitchen: scrubbed the cabinets, stocked the pantry, given everything a place. My brother had set up the office, sectioning it off from the living room with folding screens. My father was a financial advisor. He'd never worked from home before. But he still had the *big account* back in Kansas, which would keep us *out of the red* until he collected enough new business out here to justify renting a proper space.

My father yelled down from the window.

We ran upstairs.

Inside, he was standing in his boxers, just out of the shower. "Nivea me," he said.

Our job was to rub lotion all over his body.

My brother called top. I took his legs and feet.

He was like this, our dad. The television in his room and the coffeemaker in the kitchen were equipped with sleep and start timers, as if he were comforted that someone, or something, was attending to him at all times.

When we finished, he told us we were going for a drive.

"Where we headed?" I asked.

"Load 'em up, cowboys," he said.

We drove north along the foothills. My brother sat shotgun. From the backseat I stared up at the ugly mountains. The Sandias were not the great bare slabs of rock I'd imagined. I'd been disappointed to find them littered with bramble and cacti. My father veered east, up into the mountains. We were rising. I turned around. Downslope I followed the arroyo until it emptied into the Rio Grande, and farther, beyond the mountain's shrinking shadow, the earth was flat and white as paper.

"Let's air it out," my father said.

We rolled down the windows.

On the other side of Sandia Peak, along a county highway, at the far end of a little town, we came upon a rustic shack. Motorcycles filled the parking lot, twenty or so, lined up neatly like cigarettes in a fresh pack.

"Here we are, boys," my father said as he pulled in. "A real biker bar."

"Wow," I said.

"Cool," my brother said.

Nobody noticed when we walked through the door, but I pretended they did. I paid special attention to the clap of my father's soles against the worn floorboards. Last week, on a break from unpacking, my father took us to the Western Store where he bought himself his first pair of cowboy boots. Behind him now, I walked hard. We're with him, I thought.

"I'll get us some drinks," he said.

"I'll come with you," I said.

He grabbed my shoulder. "Stay here."

My brother and I sat down at a table, scanned the room. Barstool straddlers watched a baseball game on a corner set. A woman in a short skirt leaned onto the pool table, aimed her cue. Most everyone smoked, drank from bottles, sipped from short glasses. Sitting at the bar, my father had struck up conversation with a man. Our dad prided himself on his ability to float smoothly between scenes. *Social mobility*, he called it. My father stood, went to the bathroom. A few seconds later the man he was speaking with followed him. I decided to remain alert until he came back out safely.

"You think he'll let us order a beer?" my brother said.

"Ask him," I dared.

I looked at the dirt growing on his upper lip.

"What are you staring at?" he asked.

"It's just . . ." I laughed. "You look like a Mexican."

My father set down our drinks. "One Bud, one Roy Rogers, and one beer with a root to boot. Bartender says one is all we get, says I can't bring kids in here." I looked over my father's shoulder. The bartender was pointing us out to some of his patrons. My father stabbed at his chest with his thumb. "My fucking kids," he said under his breath.

He swigged back his beer, finished it. He wiped his mustache dry with his thumb and first finger. Then he sat up, scooted in, leaned onto the table. His energy sometimes changed in an instant.

"You boys know that I have a recurring dream, right? Where I'm stuck in a Spanish prison? They beat me, whip me, they threaten to crucify me."

We nodded.

"And you know that I have done extensive family re-search, I mean extensive, like really far back, to track our lineage to Spain. I still believe, truly believe, that we are of Spanish descent." He paused, considered what to say next. "Well, there's something I want you to mull over, to think about, you don't have to make your minds up right now. I don't want to offend you boys. There's nothing wrong with who we are. But I think there is something we could do to make our transition into this new place easier—a lot easier."

"Spit it out," I said.

He smiled, bit open one of his plastic-tipped cigars, lit it.

"What I want, I mean, what I'm suggesting, is that we change the pronunciation of our name to sound more Spanish. If you think about it, half my family pronounced it one way and the other half another way, so what's the harm? Who really knows, you know?"

"What would we change it to?" my brother asked.

My father called to the bartender, "Hey, pal, you got a pen?"

The bartender took his time, brought over a pen.

"You Mexican?"

"American."

"You speak Spanish though," my father said, scrawling

our last name onto a napkin, then turning the napkin to show him. "How do you pronounce this?"

The name poured from the bartender's mouth.

"Isn't that pretty?" my father asked us.

"Anything else?" the bartender said.

My father didn't respond, kept his wry eye on his kids.

"How 'bout another Bud?" he finally said.

The bartender laughed, hovered, then walked away.

"Well?" my father said to us. "What do you think?"

I'd loved the liquid way the bartender had pronounced our name. Still, the whole idea felt forced. It wasn't really necessary, was it? I thought we'd already started our lives over.

"It's a little weird," I said.

"Weird how?" my father asked.

"Well, we've been using the same last name for so long it might be hard to remember. Like at school, what if we forget and use our old name?"

He turned to my brother. "My youngest loves to pick the fly shit out of the pepper, doesn't he?"

"I don't think it's weird," my brother responded, "but it will take some adjusting."

"Everything we're doing takes adjusting," my father said. "Listen, I've always considered myself a man of routine, not of convenience. Routines can be changed. It just takes a bit of willpower. I say let's change our routine. Let's change our name. We can be whoever we want to be down here. We can all be new people." He slowed himself with a deep breath. He asked me, "Who do you want to be, son?"

That seemed like a difficult question. I didn't know how to answer.

"Christ, let me put it another way. Why did you decide to come to Albuquerque?"

"To be with you guys," my brother said.

"Me too," I said.

"You're cute," my father said to me. "Always doing what your brother's doing."

"Why did you decide to come?" I asked sharply, defending myself.

"Watch it," he warned. But it was the question he'd wanted one of us to ask. "I'm not sure you'll understand," he said, "either of you. You're not old enough. But when I was a young man, I moved out to Arizona. I traveled all over the Southwest: Santa Fe, the Rockies, southern Utah, even Mexico. There was something down here, something in the sunsets, in the mountains, the people. The Indian way of life. I call it . . . the spirit. I guess I'm returning to one of the happiest periods in my life. I am here to find the spirit again. Trust me," he suddenly implored. "Trust me. We can start over here. We have a chance to begin again. We can let go of the past. But first we need to bury the motherfucker."

The bartender was back, picking up our glasses. I wasn't finished.

My father was irritated by the interruption. He pulled a greasy menu from beneath the napkin dispenser, asked if they served food. "How about it, boys?" my father addressed us before the bartender could respond. "Want some grub?"

"Time to go," the bartender said. "I told you I wasn't serving you anything else."

"Yeah? Why's that?" my father asked him. "Why don't you tell these boys why they can't have any food. Or why you insist on disrespecting their father right in front of them."

"Why don't you tell them yourself," the bartender said. "Tell them what you really came here for." He turned to us. "Better yet, look at the way dear old dad is working the tip of that cigar. He's nearly chewed it shut."

For a quick, cutting remark my father was always reliable. Now he'd gone quiet, taken the cigar out of his mouth, hid the tip. He seemed not to know what to do with any part of his body. Why was he so wounded? What was he waiting for? It pained me to see him like this. I was frustrated by his silence, furious that the people here thought we didn't belong. We did belong. We were here—the three of us.

I turned to the bartender. "I'll have a Bud," I told him.

My father looked up.

"A Bud for me too," my brother said, following my lead.

My father grinned as he turned from us to the bartender. "Make it three," he said.

"Fuck off," the bartender said. "All of you."

On the way to the car our dad had his arms around us. "What do you say?" he asked.

"All right," my brother said, "let's bury the motherfucker."

I laughed at his opportunistic profanity.

"What about you, giggles?" my father asked me.

"Let's bury the bitch," I said. As it came out of my mouth, I suddenly realized how it sounded. I hadn't meant my mother specifically. I was only trying to be funny, to cuss like my brother had.

"Bury the bitch." My father laughed aloud. "I love that." He asked my brother, "Bury the bitch? See? I told you. Didn't I tell you? I knew your brother would come around." My father squeezed my shoulder. "It's what she gets for messing with us."

In a courtyard in the center of the little town we found the music. We sat on the edge of a paint-flecked fountain. A man strummed a Spanish guitar. My father bought his CD. The dream catchers posted next to crosses in sun-beaten doorways, the faded stucco archways, the scent of hanging chilies, the dirt, aged and covering all— I thought of my dad out here, years younger, living a happier and simpler life.

In shops we stopped to look at blankets, paintings, pottery. There were wolves, moons, lizards, cacti, oranges and yellows and browns, the strict adobe geometry. We spoke of our new home without ever mentioning the old one.

My father told us both to pick out something for the apartment.

"What are you getting?" I asked him.

He brought me to a sculpture of a woman in profile, carved from alabaster, no more than two feet tall. She was set in the reddish stone, the deepest marks revealing the alabaster's light gray core. Her hair flowed back with her dress, and her long neck leaned forward, like an animal smelling what was coming in the wind.

"Can you feel it?" my father asked.

"Yes," I said.

"She's got the spirit in her, doesn't she?" he said.

"Yes," I said.

THREE

My father was in the shower. I snagged some change from the jar on his dresser, left the apartment. I crossed the street to the bus stop. I'd never been on a city bus before, but for the past several months, because of what everyone was calling El Niño—something strange going on in Peru—I kept getting caught in a downpour on the morning walk to school. In line I followed a woman in front of me exactly: three careful steps, two quarters into the coin slot, wait for the beep. I sat down behind her. In the back, I guessed, where the noise was coming from, that was the engine.

When we neared my middle school, I stood, expecting to be let off.

We sped past. I sat down again.

Why hadn't we stopped? Was I on the wrong bus? I was too anxious to ask.

The bus finally came to a stop what seemed like several miles later. I got off. Overhead the gray sky was near, pressing close. I chose to slog to school instead of trying a different bus back.

At home that afternoon my father was waiting for me. He told me to follow him. We walked down to the Jeep, got in. He reset the odometer. We pulled out of the complex. In a few minutes we were sitting in the parking lot of my school.

"One point two miles," he said.

"Yes, but it was raining," I said.

"One point two miles."

"Yes, sir."

"No more calls from school."

"Yes, sir."

On the drive back he wore a self-approving grin, one side of his lip raised slightly, the same way he snarled. He slipped the jeep into neutral, took pleasure coasting for several blocks.

The next week the principal called again. I'd been in a fight. I hadn't been the aggressor, but in her opinion I had provoked the altercation. I'd challenged one of the better basketball players to a game during lunch and beat him bad. Then he hit me in the stomach. I was new, the principal told my father, so she was concerned. Another fight and she would have to suspend me. For now she wanted him to pick me up.

He refused.

I sat in the office until the end of the day. I used the secretary's phone to leave a message at my brother's school for him to meet me after he got out. That way no one would mess with me on my walk home. When the bell rang, he was there, waiting.

"Does Dad know?" my brother asked.

I nodded. "You think he'll be mad?"

"Your first fight, son," he impersonated our father. "You're not a child anymore. Welcome to manhood. You carry your own sins now."

"Double digits," I said, taking a turn, mimicking a talk he'd given me two years ago on my tenth birthday. "No one in our family has ever made it to triple digits."

"Six feet tall," my brother went next. "Congratulations. You're growing up so fast. You know, no one in our family has ever made it to seven feet."

"Or died a virgin," I tried.

"You might," he said.

We laughed.

Our dad was standing at the top of the stairs when we got home.

He halted my brother with his hand.

"Inside," he said to me. He ushered me into the apartment, closed the door, flicked the dead bolt. He snatched me by the neck. My body braced in fear. I fought him as he dragged me to the bathroom, where he showed me myself in the mirror. "What the fuck is the matter with you?" he hissed. He stripped his belt from the belt loops, whipped it back. After the first lash I knew my father had hit me with the buckle. After the second, my hand having reached around to block the blow, pain ripped from my finger, up my arm, into my neck. He dropped the belt, wrapped both hands around my throat. My chin tucked. Drool swung from my lip. Tears and snot ran into my mouth. He held me inches from my own reflection, threatened to smash my face. I put my hands up to the mirror to brace myself in case he tried. One of my fingernails was missing. The buckle had popped it right off. "How am I supposed to control you?" he whispered angrily into my ear. "Tell me. Is this what I have to do to get your attention? I don't know how to fucking control you. Is this how I have to do it?"

My father snarled at me through the mirror, his hot breath and wet words streaming into my ear. Then he pushed me to the floor, left me panting by the bathtub. I was horrified and confused. I'd seen him whip my mother with a belt before. In fact there were times when she was so terrorized by him that she would just give up, her entire being, like there was nothing left of her but a plea for mercy. She'd have apologized for the weather if it would have ended his rampage a second sooner. The difference was: she deserved it. What I had done paled in comparison. During their marriage she was always losing her jobs. Each new one would last a month or so before she started faking sick days without my father knowing. It infuriated him more and more every time she got fired. She pissed us kids off too. After the separation she stayed in bed all day, forgot to pay the electric bill, neglected to pick us up from school. Nights we stayed with her, my brother and I were lucky to find food in the fridge. I understood my father's frustrations with her. I shared them. Never before, though, had he handled either of us boys so violently. Until now his brutality had been reserved for her.

A few weeks later my father was in the kitchen washing dishes. He had a cigar in his mouth. Since we'd moved here, he'd taken to smoking these cheap filtered cigars all the time, as opposed to on those rare nights in Kansas. He chewed the tips until they cracked, punched them out so hard they snapped in the ashtray. It was nearly his birthday. A good cigar, I thought, would be the perfect gift.

He sensed me watching him. His eyes rolled inaccurately toward me, as if on loose bearings. He broke the silence: "How was basketball practice?"

I could tell while answering that something behind his gaze was drifting. He didn't understand what I was saying.

Or he wasn't paying attention. Or he was pretending to pay attention but was a poor actor. The ash from his cigar fell onto the plate he was scrubbing. He didn't notice. He just kept spreading the ash into the grooves of the ceramic. Then he put the plate in the dishwasher.

I asked where my brother was.

"Went to bed," he said.

"It's only seven."

Our bedroom was dark when I entered. The blinds were drawn, lights off.

"Who is that?" my brother asked.

"Me."

"Me who? Come here, Me."

I sat down on his bed. He grabbed my shoulders, pulled me close.

"Your face is a skull," he said and pushed me away.

For hours my brother tossed and turned, desperate for the mushrooms he admitted to taking after school to wear off. I'd resolved to keep to our room, take care of him until his trip passed. I sat up with him as long as I could. But I got tired and eventually dozed off. Even so, his sudden gasps of fright or wonder woke me throughout the night, and each time I'd ask if he was OK before going back to bed. When the sun was rising, I opened the blinds to clear out the darkness. He shuddered, "Close them, close them."

"I miss Kansas," I told him as I was leaving for school.

"I do too, sometimes," he said, finally falling asleep.

My father had instructed me to make friends with the biggest kid at school. Philip Olivas was high school size. Over the summer he'd been jumped by four older kids. Word was that Philip popped one of their nuts like a grape.

He said he could get me Cubans for my father's birthday.

"For real? How much are those?"

"Four for fifty."

"I just need one," I said.

"They come in fours," he said.

The next day I gave Philip all I had—forty dollars cash. And for a week he avoided me. Whenever I approached him, he'd brush me off, saying, "Chill, I'm working on it." I began to fear the worst but was also comforted when one time he went out of his way to ask, "When do you need them by? I'm sorry, man, I forgot." But then he pretended to forget again. "When's your dad's birthday? For real? Wow. Tomorrow?"

"Yes, for real. Tomorrow."

"Don't worry," he said. "I got you after school."

When the bell rang, Philip and I walked back to his house together.

In the kitchen dirty dishes covered the countertop.

Philip shooed away a cat licking the rim of a glass. A lizard ran across the wall. The cat darted for it. I asked Philip if he kept a pet lizard. "No, gringo." He smiled. I followed him to his room, where he rifled through a shelf in his closet before turning around. In his open palm I saw light green bunches with deep orange hairs, all of it frosted over.

"You spent my money on weed?"

"I'll pay you back," he said.

"What the hell am I supposed to do for my dad's birthday?"

He shrugged, asked almost politely if I wanted to get high.

"No," I said.

"Suit yourself," he said.

He banged on the wall. His older brother came into the bedroom, pipe in hand. Philip loaded it, lit it. Smoke rolled from his mouth, up his nostrils. His brother went next, took one long pull and several smaller ones. He filled his lungs and held it. Then he blew smoke in my direction.

I left soon after, not feeling a thing, thinking that, though I'd nearly thrown up from coughing and the brothers had given me enthusiastic applause, I hadn't hit the pipe properly. I walked down Philip's street. I was angry. He'd stolen my money. I had no birthday present for my dad. He would have been so happy with me. I took a deep breath, which helped me feel better. I took another. It was suddenly so easy to shrug off my disappointment. Looking up: cartoon clouds. The sky had such color, shape, dimension. A half-mile ahead, in the park behind our apartment, the tops of trees were swaying in a high breeze. I felt the urge to hear a branch break, wood crack. I popped my knuckles close to my ear and giggled. For the first time in my life I was high.

Across the street from our complex I waited for the light to change.

"Let's just hope Dad's not home," I said aloud.

In the parking lot the Jeep was nowhere to be found.

I shot up the stairs to the apartment.

Inside, there was a Post-it note on his bedroom door: "Went Out. Do not enter."

I fell onto the couch, embraced my victory. I got lost observing the reflection of my thin, alien silhouette in the television. I picked up the remote control, turned the TV on, turned it off again. I was starving. I needed money. I stood, tried my father's door. It was locked. I grabbed the toolbox. One of the smaller Allen wrenches fit perfectly into the tiny hole. The lock clicked. I opened the door, went to his dresser to grab change from the jar.

His voice cut through the stillness.

I jumped. My heart raced. I turned to my father. He had a metal pipe in his hand, and just behind him on the nightstand there was a plate of white powder, a box of baking soda, a lighter, a spoon. The fear of punishment consumed me. I'd broken my father's golden rule—privacy. I hadn't just broken it either. I knew instantly that I'd discovered the reason the rule existed. I looked away, not wanting him to think I'd seen anything. Then I turned, my head still down, and walked out of his bedroom, closing the door behind me.

I sat down on the couch.

He was going to send me back to Kansas. He was going to march out of his room and tell me that I had to go live with my mother. I was never really one of the boys, he'd say. I didn't belong here. He'd given me a chance, and I'd blown it. I couldn't be trusted. He'd call me an *Amalekite*—the nickname he used for my mother. He'd need to be rid of me like he'd needed to be rid of her. My mind rushed to the Polaroids. They are in a neat stack on the table. The social worker shows me one at a time. "Yes," I say, "my mom did this." She asks me why the handprints on my face look fresh when the pictures had been taken several hours after she'd hit me. I don't have an answer. She doesn't believe me. She leaves the room. Behind the two-way mirror in the wall I hear her talking to another woman.

"What else?" the other voice asks. "Did his mother do anything else?"

Back in the room the woman asks, "Did your mother do anything else?"

This time I'm prepared. I'm not going to disappoint my father. It's my responsibility to get us free. "There was this one night," I tell the social worker, "I was staying at my mom's apartment. I had a nightmare, and I went to her room and woke her up." I pause, pretend that this is hard for me. It's not. It's easy. "I know I'm a little old for that," I go on. "It was a terrible dream though. I told her I was scared, and she said I could sleep with her. Well, we fell back asleep all right, but when I woke up like an hour later . . ." I pause again, rub my eyes. "My mom's hand was down my boxers. She was touching me, like stroking. It was weird. I mean, I didn't even really understand what she was doing. She'd never done anything like that before. I almost didn't believe it was happening. I didn't know what to do either. So I rolled onto my stomach, away from her, and I just lay there for a while until I felt it was safe to sneak back to my room."

"Hush, now," my father told me. "Hush."

He'd come out of his bedroom, found me on the carpet, my hands around my knees, rocking, crying. I'd somehow slid down the edge of the couch.

"It's all right," he said. "Stop. Please, just stop."

31

"I lied to them, Dad," I told him. "You can't send me back."

"I know, son. I know. It's OK. You did what you had to do. You got us free."

He was petting the back of my head.

"You knew?" I said.

"I'm proud of you."

"I'm on your team. I chose you."

"Stop, please. You're not in trouble. Hush. Quiet now."

His commands were irresistible. They soothed me.

"Don't be mad," I said. "I only wanted some change for a sandwich."

He reached into his pocket, pulled out his money clip, handed me a ten.

"Split a tuna with me," he said.

He helped me up, walked me to the door.

"What do you want on it?" I asked.

"Whatever you want," he said.

He was so good to us sometimes.

On my way to the grocery store, at the opposite end of the parking lot, a hundred yards from our apartment, I happened by the Jeep. My father had hidden our car to back up the Post-it note. When I returned with the sandwich, he was in his room again, a sour, chemical smell coming from under his door. I ended up splitting the tuna with my brother that night. I told him about the social worker in Kansas. And what I'd seen today in our dad's bedroom. He already knew I had lied to CPS. Our father had sworn him to secrecy. He then recounted a fight he'd overheard between our parents, during which our mom had threatened to tell everyone about the drugs. "I didn't know what she was talking about," my brother said. "I thought she was making it up."

Two days passed. My father didn't leave his room. He spent his birthday in there. He emerged on Sunday. My brother and I were on the couch watching TV. He called a meeting.

"Boys," he began, "I'm sure you've noticed I act strange sometimes."

"We already know, Dad," my brother interrupted.

"What do you know?"

"You get high." I couldn't believe my brother just said it.

"You know shit is what you know. Turn off the television."

"We already know, Dad," I said, backing up my brother.

"Yes, well, you boys are smart. I trained you that way." He stretched the *I* as long as he could. "But you don't know everything."

"It's OK, Dad," my brother said.

33

"I want to come clean. Can I come clean?" He looked around like he was addressing a larger audience. "It's my turn to talk. I called this meeting." He started again. "The sixties were a crazy time. I'd go to wine tastings with colleagues. It was a social routine. Well, everyone there used to smoke pot. It was the thing to do. The marijuana brings out the particularities in the wine. Different smells and tastes. Different notes. I guess I've been doing it ever since. Not that frequently though. It's nothing serious, nothing you need to worry about. Just a little reefer is all." He waited for us to respond. We sat there in silence. "We are all entitled to one bad habit, aren't we? Aren't we? You guys have bad habits too. You pop your knuckles, don't you?" he asked me.

"Yes," I said.

"You understand then?" he said, shaking his head in relief. "I swear you two never cease to amaze me. Such precocious boys. I feel better now that you know. It's a real load off." He closed his eyes, nodded emphatically.

"Thanks for being honest," my brother said.

"That's it! The great thing about honesty. It's a release."

He opened his arms wide, gestured with flicks of his fingers for us to give him a hug. We walked over. He put his arms around us.

"You boys understand the importance of telling each other the truth, right?"

"Of course," my brother said.

"Family is all we have," my father said.

"Yes," I agreed. "Family is all we have."

FOUR

He stared blankly into the frying pan, stirring the eggs, waiting for them to cook. He still had not realized the burner was off. Before, he'd been at the countertop buttering bread until the centers gave out. He was trying to act normal, make his kids breakfast before school. His scruff was long, hair matted. The capillaries in his eyes were exposed wires. He had not slept for days. He was still in last week's clothes. At the table my brother and I ate cereal, watched him, exchanged smirks.

For the most part I liked it when my father was high. He was soft, restrained, subdued. He would shuffle across the room barely lifting his feet or just gaze out the window for hours. I now understood that all those times back in Kansas when he would suddenly send us out of the house he'd actually been wanting to do drugs. He'd give us money, tell us to ride our bikes to the 7-Eleven, and when we returned with our Slurpees, the blinds would be drawn and he'd be docile. Those nights my brother and

I would play football in the street until after dark. We'd order in, watch TV, stay up as late as we liked. My father would call a cab to take us to school the next morning or to bring us home after. I hadn't made sense of any of this until I walked in on him a month ago. I'd just figured he trusted us to take care of ourselves.

His routine went something like: after about a week of him getting high in his bedroom, cigars no longer masking the other smoke, he'd crash, sleep a full day. The second day of the comedown, step lightly—he was a bear. And everyday after, he was more recognizably our dad. He'd make it to meals, basketball games, and on Saturdays, he would even take us out to the court in the park behind our apartment. There, he'd pit my brother and me against each other, refusing to ever call a foul. The downside to the drugs, though, was when he fell behind on his work. My brother would have to stay home from school to file, pay bills, reach out to potential clients, and over the past few weeks he'd missed several basketball practices. Coach Baez was a spiteful man. As punishment he forced my brother to watch while the rest of the team ran suicides for his absences.

When we finished breakfast, my brother stole away to our bedroom. I washed his bowl, packed both of our lunches. I tiptoed around the stove, not wanting to break my father's concentration. I was helping my brother make a clean getaway.

On our way out the door my father stopped him. "Need you today."

"I have a game tomorrow," my brother pleaded. "Coach has already warned me."

"I'll stay," I volunteered.

My father shook his head.

My brother dropped his school bag.

After a few hours of work my father gave him cash, sent him to the movies. He drove to school instead, late for fifth-period practice. "It was the big account," my brother told me that night when I asked him how his coach had reacted. "What the fuck was I supposed to do?"

My brother didn't play the next day, and not for several games after. I watched them all from the bleachers. My father sometimes came along. Each game, up until the final buzzer, my brother remained alert on the bench, feet bouncing. Baez ignored him.

The next time he played was weeks later out on the west side in Rio Rancho. I rode the bus with the team. My brother and I sat near the front. He didn't talk to any of his teammates. Raucous in the back, they didn't talk to him either. I wondered if my brother had trouble making new friends too. I hated my middle school. I'd been made fun of ever since my dad forced me to run for student council. I knew it was a bad idea, but he had insisted, citing his own junior high résumé. I gave my speech after my opponent—a pretty blond cheerleader. My father had instructed that I start off with an apology for not doing whatever flashy thing he knew she would do. When I told the student body that I had not brought in a putter to symbolize the hole-in-one I would sink when under pressure or a baseball bat to represent the home run I'd hit in my duties, someone in the crowd yelled, "That's 'cause you suck." After laughter another said, "You're not in Kansas anymore, faggot." Then, a popular kid, Kyle, who'd sworn he'd vote for me, stood up and suggested that I try to poop out of my butt chin. At home that night I'd reported a near-victory to my father. Now on the bus I was surprised to learn that my brother wasn't more popular. He was the obvious heir to our dad's easy charm.

In the second quarter Baez finally put him in. My brother seized the opportunity. He danced through the defense, got to the basket with ease, scored in bunches. Rio Rancho's coach had no choice but to double him. My brother then dished out bunnies to his teammates, open jump shots and easy layups. He made Baez look like a fool. His teammates must have felt like asses for shunning him.

That's my brother, I wanted to yell. How good is he? How dumb are all of you? This is what you've been missing.

At halftime my father walked into the gym. My brother had heard him wandering through the apartment late last night. I'd heard him the night before. He was in one of his cycles. We'd figured him for a no-show. I waved to him. He waved back. His sagging pants sagged lower. His shirt was wrinkled with only the front tucked in, as if he thought he could not be seen from the back. As if he imagined himself two-dimensional.

He sat down next to me.

"Bright in here," I said.

He kept his sunglasses on.

"What'd I miss?" he asked.

It rushed out of me, every detail. I told him how amazing my brother had been. I even used my father's nickname for him, *Silk*, a moniker I'd always envied. My father nodded, or did not. His head tilted a bit, which meant something, or nothing. His spine, I hoped, would snap from the weight of his skull slowly lolling back.

"You have . . . white stuff," I said, pointing to the corner of my lip.

The buzzer sounded. The teams returned from their locker rooms. As he ran out to the court, my brother looked to the stands. I knew he was wanting to share with me a sly grin. Instead he turned away, head down, embarrassed.

41

He'd seen who I was sitting with. For the first time all season my brother started the third quarter. The rest of the game he did not score a single point.

On the ride home my father pulled the car over to the side of the road, dry heaved.

"Bad pizza," he said.

"Case closed," my brother said.

My brother took over driving duties. My father moved to shotgun.

My brother continued his story. "You know what Baez asked me at halftime?"

"What?" I said.

"He wanted to know if I'd eaten pussy before the game."

We both laughed.

My father mumbled something.

"What's that?" my brother asked.

"Son of a bitch," my father said.

"Who?" I asked.

"Little Caesar," my brother said.

"Papa John," I said.

"What is he talking about?" my brother asked me.

That was all my father said on the subject until later that week, the second day of his comedown. My brother and I were on the couch, quiet, vigilant, nodding in agreement as our dad paced around the apartment, ranting, "You don't take a player out of his game. You don't psych a player out like he psyched you out. No wonder you went cold after half. That's not how you coach. Nothing. Nothing. Nothing. You pretend like nothing happened until after the game. You don't mention it, Baez. You go about business as usual, you son of a bitch."

"You," my father said to me as I was leaving for school. "You're staying home today."

My brother had already said no, left hastily.

"Me?"

"This concerns you."

"The big account?"

"Something like that."

I dropped my bag. "How can I help?"

He'd shaved, combed his hair. Sober and *suited up*—the phrase he used whenever he put on a jacket and tie—he spread his arms wide. "You can come here and give your father a hug."

That afternoon, from the parking lot of Rio Rancho High, way out on the west side, my father and I looked to the Sandias. At this distance the mountains were a faint and purple hump beneath a pale blue sky.

The coach stood up from his desk when we walked into his office.

"Thanks for calling ahead," he said. We sat down. "So, Kansas?"

"Kansas."

"And when you moving to New Mexico?"

"This coming school year."

My father had not prepped me. It was a test. He wanted to see if I was savvy enough to figure this situation out on my own. It was obvious. He was going to transfer us to a new school district. I loved the idea. In a year and a half I wanted to start high school without anyone remembering me. My brother, I figured, would also be grateful for a change of scenery. But why was my dad pretending we didn't live in New Mexico already? Just tell the coach about my brother, remind him. Wasn't that the dealmaker?

Either way, it didn't matter. My job here was simple: follow my father's lead.

"How many players you got for me?" the coach asked.

"Two blue chips." My father pointed to me. "This one'll be ready in a couple years."

The coach eyed me skeptically. I wasn't nearly as good as my brother, not nearly as physically developed either. I sat up as tall as I could, clenched my jaw, tried to make myself look older than I was. "Well," he said, "let's see what he can do."

The coach ran me through one-on-one drills, cone dribbling, spot-up shooting. At one point I dribbled the ball off my foot. And later he corrected my shooting form, said I needed to learn to release the ball with one hand, not two. I wasn't doing as well as I'd hoped. I was letting the boys down. My father was relying on me. My brother too.

We ended with free throws.

"Ten of them," the coach said.

I made all ten.

"Shoot till you miss," he said.

Fifty-two free throws later, the coach smiled at my father. "If it ain't broke."

"You should see his older brother," my father said.

"Yes," he said. "I think I should."

Outside Rio Rancho High the day shimmered. The sun seemed endless and the land level. My father insisted on holding my hand on the way to the car. He was proud of me. I'd stepped up, sunk more free throws in a row than either of us had thought possible. We spent hours exploring the west side. At a restaurant we split a giant burrito, and when the waitress asked, "Red or green chili," my father answered, "Christmas." We looked at model homes and small plots in a new development. We decided on the flat-roof, one-story Pueblo-style with stucco siding, round-edged walls, and heavy timber jutting the front face. My father told the agent that he'd have to crunch some numbers. I knew that meant we couldn't afford it, but I also hoped maybe we could. We left with a brochure.

After school my brother flew into the apartment, screaming. Rio Rancho's coach had recognized our last name and called Baez to confirm. My brother had been forced to plead with his coach that he'd had no role in the plot. Baez didn't believe him. He called him a traitor, told him he wouldn't play another minute the rest of the season. Next year too, Baez warned, good luck making the team.

I listened to them argue from our bedroom.

"If your coach wants war, we'll give it to him," my father said. "As long as you're on that team, you can collect information to share with Rio Rancho. It makes you more of an asset when you transfer. This is a perfect exit strategy."

"I don't want an exit strategy. I don't want to move. Why can't we just stay still?"

"I thought you would've been happy. We did this for you."

My brother threatened to quit.

At that my father backpedaled, apologized. The truth was: he loved that my brother was always the best player on the court. It gave him a sense of importance—leverage with coaches, status in the stands. He promised that he'd make it right with Baez. He'd call him personally to take the blame. I was heartbroken. My father succumbed so easily. He left out all of the details of our day together. He let go of our hope for a house, for a new beginning. And my brother refused to see the benefits of Rio Rancho. He was being stubborn for no reason. The joy of today gone, I felt alone in our bedroom. I was furious at them both.

I stood a little away from my father, embarrassed by his desperation. He was a few days into his comedown, still too volatile to be trusted. He was waiting outside the locker room after a game, ready to force Baez into a conversation. It had been weeks. Coach had refused to respond to my father's phone calls. My brother, as promised, had not played a minute since.

The team came out of the locker room. Coach Baez walked right past my father, ignored him when he asked for a word in private. My father grabbed his shoulder. Baez pointed a finger in my father's face, then went to walk away. My father shoved him from behind. The whole team watched as Baez slammed into the bleachers, pushed back off, turned, and punched my father in the nose. He fell on his ass, his legs splayed out in front of him. He looked around the gymnasium, stunned, an infant about to bawl, bleeding all over his shirt. I waited for my father to stand so as not to embarrass him further. I followed him to the bathroom, helped clean him up.

At home, the lower rims of his eye sockets bruised, my

father told my brother that there was still hope. After today, though, he would have to transfer. My brother had no other choice, my father explained. I grabbed the brochure from the Rio Rancho development, took the opportunity to sell him on the move. I pointed out the model home we liked, told him about the amenities we could choose from. I even mentioned the morning deck, the one that faced the mountains, the sunrise.

"Let me call Rio Rancho's coach," my father said. "Just give me the go-ahead."

My brother got up, went to our room without saying a word.

In bed that night I asked him what he thought about the house in the brochure.

"We can't afford any of that shit, dumbass."

"Fine," I fired back. "Then what are you going to do about Baez?"

He ignored me.

"Your coach hit Dad in the face," I said. "Aren't you going to do anything?"

The next day he quit the team.

Out in the park on Saturday my brother lowered his shoulder into my chest, knocked me to the ground, went in for a layup. My father, per usual, said nothing.

On my first possession I pulled up for a jump shot.

My brother flicked me in the balls.

I called a foul.

"No fouls," my brother said.

My father kept silent.

My brother grinned at us both.

He didn't care about what was fair. He was making his own rules to his own game. He was going after me to get back at our dad. Maybe he was angry with me, too. He took the ball, ran me over a second time, but rather than score a basket he dribbled back out to the three-point line, waited for me to get up. I got up. He knocked me to the ground again, and again I was up, my elbows and palms scraped raw. It didn't matter why my father was not intervening. I didn't want him to anymore. And it wasn't about Rio Rancho either. I was done being ignored, pushed around. I'd only tried to do right by the two of them, and I was getting bullied for it. My brother came at me once more, shoulder lowered. This time I was ready. I sidestepped, stuck my leg out to trip him. This is what you get, I thought, both of you. You can hurt me, but I can hurt you, too.

My brother hopped over my foolish leg, drove to the hole, laid the ball softly into the net. He was such a beautiful basketball player. It was a marvel to watch him move.

* * *

My father sat us down for another of his family meetings later that day. "Listen," he said, "I'm not proud of how I've treated you boys since we've been here. I've been inconsistent. I've made mistakes. We came here together, each of our own volition, for our own reasons, to start a new life. It hasn't been easy, true. As the father, that makes me the leader, so some of it is my fault." He looked to my brother. "If it's important to you to stay at your school, I understand. But are you sure that's what you want?" My brother lied, said he didn't care about basketball, he just didn't want to move again. "I respect that. Lord knows, my father moved us around to a new school every year. There is virtue in sticking it out, in staying put, in building the stamina necessary to endure anything. We can take it. Can't we take it? Can't we?"

We nodded.

"Good. There's something else that I want to say. Me and my little brother, Donny, your uncle Don, we were never close. We were eight years apart. He was my father's favorite. I was my mom's. Anyway, I never wanted that for you. That's why I had you boys two years apart. It was my idea to have both of you, you know? Well, actually," he said to my brother, "your mother must have been putting the birth control up the wrong hole with you." He waited for us to smile at his joke. He turned to me. "But you, you were my idea. You wouldn't exist without me. You boys, you're so close in age, you're supposed to be there for each other. You're supposed to stand up for each other no matter what. You understand, don't you? Don't you? Don't look at me. What are you looking at me for? Look at your brother. Look at your brother, damn it." We turned to each other. "This is your brother for life. You are his last line of defense."

FIVE

I waited for my brother outside the grocery store where he
worked, across the street from our apartment. I'd already
slipped in, moseyed past his register. He would then slip
out, hand off razorblades, deodorant, toothbrushes he'd
stolen for us. He figured passing this stuff to me was
safer than carrying it out at the end of his shift. I didn't
mind—we were in cahoots. Besides, I hadn't seen him
much lately. He'd been working doubles five days a week
since summer began. "Business has been slow," our dad
had told us when the school year ended. "You boys need
to carry the weight these next few months." Too young
to work legally, I had answered a want ad for an old lady
who needed help organizing a lifetime of miscellanea. On
payday my brother and I signed over our checks.

My brother came out, handed me a pack of gum.

"Why aren't you at work?" he said.

"Doris's car is in the shop."

"Dad couldn't drive you?"

"I told him yesterday that I needed a ride, but his door is still closed."

"Any smoke yet?"

I nodded.

"You get a day off then, huh?" he said. "Lucky you."

My brother stared into a bright puddle, the light reflecting in his eyes. The rain had stopped only moments before. He looked to the sky where the clouds were thinning before the sun. Then he checked out my swim trunks.

"You going to the pool?"

"What gave you that idea?"

He smiled.

"I got to get back to work," he said. "Somebody's got to."

He went in through the sliding doors.

I was surprised to find anyone at the pool on a weekday, but our neighbors from downstairs, Sandy and Amelia, both in their late twenties, were talking to Mr. Aguilar who lived right next door to us. Barrel-chested, with a shaven face and closely cropped hair, he looked like a military man in his high-waisted swim trunks. We exchanged smiles, waves. I toed the water, dived in, smoothly grazed my chest along the pool floor before kicking my way back to the surface. I swam around, occasionally staring up at the mountains, grateful to have a day to myself.

Mr. Aguilar called to me.

I swam over, a side crawl.

"These girls think you're cute," he said, nodding toward Sandy.

"Thanks," I said. I glanced at them both quickly. I thought about making out with Lindsay, this girl from school, in the movie theater a few months ago. My father always said that women can sense who's *getting the smooey*. I rested my forearms on the edge of the pool, looked at the cement a few feet in front of me, searched for something to say. I saw their cooler. "What are you drinking?"

"Bloody Mary. You want one, sweetie?" Sandy asked.

"Can I try yours?"

She leaned forward on her lounge chair, swung the cup to me. I took a slow sip. The spice caught in the back of my throat. "I think I'm OK," I said, coughing.

They all laughed.

"You want a beer, buddy?" Mr. Aguilar asked. "Come on," he said to Amelia. "Let's get some more ice and our young buck here a beer."

Amelia looked at me. "You want a beer, babe?"

I shrugged. "Why not?"

I pushed back from the edge, sank into the water. The alcohol was warming my body from the inside. My veins felt as though they were expanding. I could see Sandy lowering herself gradually into the pool. Her legs looked amputated and swollen below the waterline, her large chest

55

swaying above it. She slipped in all the way, submerged herself. We floated up to the surface together.

"They'll be gone for a little while," Sandy said.

"Why's that?"

"I think they went back for more than ice, you know? Might as well have some fun on our day off. She's had a crush on him for a while. How about you? Summer vacation?"

I said yes.

"High school?"

"I'll be a freshman," I lied. "Where do you guys work?"

"Gals."

"What?"

"Gals. We are women. I'm sure you noticed."

I stole a glance at her breasts resting on the water. I was sure she noticed. I looked up at her face again. The pool water had made her mascara run. The black streaks reminded me of my mother. She and my father, they are upstairs in their bedroom, fighting. The door is closed. My father's furious. She's lost another job. My brother and I blame her for having outraged him, for breaking the peace in the house. We decide to ambush her when she comes out of their bedroom. We tie sewing thread at ankle height around the banister outside their door, Scotch tape it to the wall. We place Hot Wheels on each stair step in case she escapes the trip wire. We wait in the hallway bathroom with cups of water we plan to douse her with once she tumbles down the stairs. Then we will berate her, tell her that she is a bad wife, a shitty mom, that she's ruined our lives.

The tape rips easily from the wall when she runs from the bedroom. She doesn't notice as on her way down the stairs she steps on a Hot Wheel. She moves quickly, her head down, hands over face. At the bottom of the stairs my brother and I call to her softly, as rehearsed. When she looks up, her cheeks smeared with mascara, there is the reflex of contrition in her eyes. Her mouth is already forming the words *I'm sorry*. We throw water in her face. "You bitch," we say. "Fuck you. We hate you." She runs faster down the next flight. We look to our dad standing at the top of the stairs. What have you done? he seems to be asking. He chases after her. Out in the driveway she struggles to unlock the car door. He apologizes, puts his arms around her. He loves her, he tells her, "They didn't mean it, come back inside." She sways in his arms. They slow dance before a broad blue sky. As they turn, I notice a gash on the back of my mother's head. He must have ripped out a chunk of her hair.

I dipped down into the water, spun around, came back up.

"Where do you gals work?" I asked.

* * *

Sandy was sunning in her chair, eyes closed, back arched. Her legs were glazed in spray lotion. I'd been peeking at them from the pool.

"You going to drift around all day or you want this beer?" Mr. Aguilar said.

He waded over to me, elbows above water, hands holding two beers in koozies. I cracked mine open, took a sip. The beer tasted like dirty water. I took another quick sip. I could feel my veins expanding again.

"I'll tell you." He shook his head in astonishment.

I wanted him to say more, but he didn't.

He asked me if I'd kept Sandy company.

"We talked for a little while."

"Why the hell is she sitting over there all alone?"

"I ran out of things to say."

"How old are you? Never mind. Just stay close." He swung around. I followed him to where Sandy and Amelia now sat, their feet dangling in the water. "Ladies," he proclaimed, "your knights have returned."

"Hello, men," Sandy said. "Welcome back."

Amelia eyed Mr. Aguilar, seductively or angrily, I wasn't sure. He put his hands on her thighs, his fingers pressing into her skin. He buried his head between her legs, right in her crotch, shook side to side. The girls laughed. I felt like I shouldn't be watching, and I looked to Sandy for escape. She winked.

"Let's play a game," she said. "Let's go around the circle and all tell a secret. How about our most recent sexual experience?"

"Let's not play this game," Amelia insisted.

"Come on," Sandy said.

"Why not?" Mr. Aguilar asked. "Unless you're embarrassed that twenty minutes ago we were doing the horizontal bop?"

Amelia hit him on the arm, smirked. He nodded to me. Was it my turn? Or was he just being friendly?

"Girls your age sprouting tits yet?" Mr. Aguilar asked me. He grabbed one of Sandy's boobs. "Not like these beauties I bet."

Amelia smacked him, less playfully this time and right across the face.

"We're just having fun," Sandy said in his defense.

Amelia didn't seem that upset. The slap was more of an instinct. She put her hand up to his face to rub away the red. "I'm sorry, baby," she said.

Sandy looked at me, a corner of her mouth rising. It was my turn. I only had one story. I pictured myself again with Lindsay, my hand up her shirt. She'd tried to reach into my pants, but I got nervous, faked a stomachache. The next day at school she told everyone that I was a prude. She hadn't spoken to me since.

I took another swig of my beer.

"It's OK," Sandy said. "I'll go first."

I cut her off. "I got a blowjob at the movies last week."
I wished I'd said it slower.

"Does that happen often?" Sandy asked.

"At the movies?"

"Blowjobs."

"All the time," I said with ease, nailing it. "I get blowjobs all the time."

"How old are you again?" Mr. Aguilar asked. He
slapped me on the back, called me an early bloomer.

"And you?" I said to Sandy. "What's your story?"

She took her time before answering. I sipped my beer
to break from her stare.

"Last week," she began, "I came to the pool by myself.
It was nighttime, around ten or eleven. No one was here.
I swam around for a little while. The cold water gave me
chicken skin, made my nipples hard." She closed her eyes,
touched her breasts lightly. "At some point I felt the water
jets against my thigh and got the idea to put myself up to
one of them." She moved her hand down her stomach,
opened her eyes, smiled at Amelia. "Never in my life have
I come like that."

"Good goddamn," shouted Mr. Aguilar. "Now that's
fucking showmanship."

The rain started with a drizzle. Dark clouds had swept
in from the south.

"Let's go," Amelia said.

"You come too," Sandy said to me.

On the way to our building, at Amelia's coaxing, Mr. Aguilar dropped back to talk to me. She and Sandy walked a few paces in front of us.

"Hey, bubba," he said. "Where's your head at?"

"They're talking about me."

"All good things, I'm sure."

"I don't think Amelia likes me."

"She likes you fine."

I heard Amelia raise her voice. "He lives right above us with his fucking dad."

To whatever Sandy said next, Amelia threw her hands down, conversation over.

From the couch, Amelia's door cracked, I could see her and Mr. Aguilar making out on the bed. He was on top. She clung to him like a tree dweller. Sandy had run off to the shower. She'd given me a fresh beer, told me to sit tight.

The room had gradually darkened. Rain pelted down outside, battering the pavement. I sat there thinking about the memory I'd recalled earlier at the pool. I grimaced at the image of the red raw spot on the back of my mother's head. I couldn't comprehend how we'd ever thought up that plan. Where had it come from? The answer was obvious: our loyalty had always been to our dad. He was stronger. We feared him. He needed us. His approval always meant so much more than hers—it filled me up.

I took a sip of my beer and felt even worse.

I put the can down on the coffee table, got up to check the windows.

"Thanks, sweetie," Amelia said. "I was just coming out here to do that."

She scooted past me, closed the bottom pane. Then she climbed onto the arms of the recliner, reached up to lock the top. Mr. Aguilar peeked his head out of her bedroom, hushed me with a finger, crept over to her. He pulled down her bikini bottoms. He smacked her, bit her.

"Stop, you dog." She was laughing. "You're going to make me fall."

She jumped down from the chair, pulled her bottoms back up. They kissed. She said she was going to hop in the shower. When she was gone, Mr. Aguilar tossed a condom onto the seat cushion next to me. I stared at it, marking its resemblance to the free suckers I used to get at the bank.

"You need more than one?"

"You really think she wants to have sex with me?"

"You've never done it before?" I shook my head. "You got curly hairs, don't you?" I nodded. He thought for a moment. "Once you start kissing, tell her she's beautiful. She'll take care of the rest."

"How do I get her to kiss me?" I asked.

"You got about as much sense as two monkeys fucking a football."

He jumped up suddenly, disappeared into Sandy's room.

A moment later he led her to the living room by the hand.

"Look at this beautiful woman," he said.

He ripped off her towel, spun her around slowly, showed her to me.

I looked at her body. Her damp brown hair was combed back behind her shoulders and drops of water dripped between her legs onto the carpet. Her breasts were big, full, falling slightly to the side over her ribs. Her stomach drooped. Her belly button looked folded over on itself. Her pubic hair was trimmed into a sharp triangle. Her legs were short, stubby, proportional. She was unembarrassed, naked to the world, the first woman I had ever seen.

"Damn, she's hot," Mr. Aguilar said.

Then he turned her to him and kissed her.

It didn't take much of an excuse. I told them I needed to make sure the windows were closed in my apartment, and I didn't come back. Upstairs, my father's door was shut, smoke seeping out from under it. But he had drawn the living room blinds since I'd left this morning. The gray light that managed its way inside made everything look old. My brother was still at the grocery store. He'd be there till closing. I sat down to watch TV. My father came out a moment later, struggling to relight his cigar. His shirt was stained, his khakis frayed at the cuffs. He looked up at me, the whites of his eyes a pale orange, as if the blood in his body had dimmed, died a little. He puttered over to his desk, sat down, pretended he'd been working all day.

"You off early?" he asked.

"I didn't have a ride, remember?"

"Everybody works in this house," he warned. "What've you been up to?"

I told him what had happened at the pool in a way that would make him proud. How I'd flirted with Sandy, how I'd made her want me, that Mr. Aguilar and Amelia had already had sex, that I'd seen Sandy naked, and that Mr. Aguilar was one floor below us, right now, with both of them. He went to his room, put on clean pants, a collared shirt, closed-toed shoes. He combed his mustache, opened his cologne and sprayed some *foofoo*. He went to the kitchen, where he took a shot of the peppermint schnapps he stored in the freezer. All the while a grotesque grin had stretched his face. His feet moved in shuffles across the carpet to the front door, and he walked out.

*   *   *

My father woke me late that night. "Be my eyes," he whispered. I climbed from bed, crept to the window, careful not to wake my brother. My job now was to keep watch for fifteen or twenty minutes, look for movement: car, person, anything. I sat there for a while. Lightning cut down in the distance behind the Sandias, hewing the mountains out of the darkness. I used to cherish these nights back in Kansas when my father would wake me from the dead of sleep, and after playing lookout I'd go downstairs to the den (the hallway mirror removed from the wall or covered with a sheet) and allay his paranoia. I'd never told my brother about any of this. It was a task, I believed, that our father had chosen specifically for me, something he knew only I could do. This was a duty, I was certain, he'd assigned to me because of my potential for loyalty, for secrecy.

I walked out to the living room.

"No activity," I reported.

He thanked me, said to go to bed. Then he told me to stop. He stood there, staring blankly out the window to the park, his underwear illuminated by the bright night sky. He'd calmed. I'd done that for him. I could feel his gentleness now. "Tomorrow," he said, almost tenderly, "I'm going up to the complex to tell them what kind of white trash we have living in this building. That'll teach the three of them to fuck with us again."

SIX

I asked my brother if he thought our dad was high.

"Yes," he said.

"Good," I said.

We were coming back from the Laundromat, trash bags of clean clothes in hand, returning to our new apartment, at the opposite end of the complex. For the same price as the old, plus two months free, my father had leveraged the rental office to give us a bigger unit (first floor, back porch, still with a view of the park) as far as possible from Mr. Aguilar and the girls.

At the front door my brother asked if it was locked or unlocked.

It was my turn to guess, his turn to ask.

"Locked," I said.

He set down his bags, checked. It was locked.

"Remember," he said, curling his arm into a muscle, "the harder you hit me, the harder I hit you next time." I felt puny next to him. He'd filled out since we'd moved here, his biceps much bigger than mine. His shirts barely fit anymore. At least I was in line to inherit some of his old stuff. He was going to have to ask our dad for new clothes. I noticed a hole in his collar, tried to finger it.

"Don't make it worse," he snapped.

I called him a sore loser, punched him as hard as I could.

"You hit like a girl," he said.

My brother pulled out his key, unlocked the door. It opened only a few inches before stopping abruptly. My father had installed a chain lock. He let us in a moment later. Inside, the apartment was dark. Smoke swirled in beams of daylight shooting through the cracks in the blinds. Two girls not much older than my brother were sitting on the couch. The one nearest us smiled. She was in her bra. The other said something in Spanish in the direction of my father's room. A guy about the same age as the girls came out.

"Let's get some air in here," my father said.

He motioned the girls into his room, closed the door behind the four of them.

We set down the laundry. My brother went to open the windows. I dabbed out a cigar burning in the ashtray, then collected cocktail glasses.

"Who are they?" I asked him.

"How the fuck should I know?"

"How old are they?"

He didn't know that either.

In our room I pointed to my brother's bed.

"Motherfucker," he said.

"More like daughterfucker," I said.

With a tissue my brother removed a condom from his sheets.

My father knocked on our door a few minutes later, waited for us to invite him in. But for a few silver hairs his stubble was long and black and crept up to his cheekbones. He needed a shave. He was restless. Random muscles fired with a sudden unstable energy. He chewed the chain of his necklace, the Kokopelli pendant anchored somewhere in his shirt.

"I need you to take my friends home," he told my brother.

"I'm going with him," I said.

"No, I need you." He turned to my brother again. "And you, be back in ten."

My brother took the keys, stormed out.

I followed my father. Since we'd moved to this apartment, my brother and I had not been allowed to enter his bedroom. We hadn't even helped him set it up. Now inside, I saw that his bed was neatly made, blanket tucked at the corners. The paintings of adobe dwellings he'd had in his room in our last apartment were leaning against the wall, still to be hung. Aside from a glass of water on his bedside table there was little proof that someone lived here. The drawers might have been bare. He began to undress.

"Give me a five-minute warning," he said.

"Are we going somewhere?" I asked.

I walked into his bathroom, turned the shower to his preferred temperature. My job was to alert him five minutes after he'd gotten in. I took a moment to check for evidence. His wastebasket was empty. The toilet seat was down, sink top clear. I could see beneath his bed from where I stood. Nothing there either. He'd covered his tracks.

"Are we going somewhere?" I asked again, walking out of the bathroom.

My dad stood there naked, wild-looking. His skin was ashy. His chest hair was gray. His stomach shrunken, testicles low. A deep breath revealed more rib than I'd remembered. "If Janice calls," he said, "tell her we'll be over shortly."

In the kitchen I rinsed out the glasses. I scrubbed the spoons I found in the sink. The burn marks did not come out. They were all like that. On the countertop there was a white powder. I touched it with my finger, put some up to my nose, sneezed. I wiped up the baking soda with a sponge. Who were those girls? And that guy? I looked at the clock. How long had my brother been gone already? I opened the front door to hear the rumble of the Jeep

70

whenever he returned. Then I went to put away our clean clothes.

The phone rang. It was Janice. I told her that we'd be over shortly.

"Coming over?" she said. "No, not today. I told your father that he can come by anytime tomorrow. Please tell him again. Or just have him call me, OK? Today is no good. He knows this."

My father had picked up Janice a month or so ago, across the street at the grocery store where my brother worked. He'd spotted her in the frozen food section, sent me on a scouting mission to check her ring finger for a *ROG-er*, a *Ring of Gold*.

"Negative on that ROG-er, Dodger," I'd reported back.

"Hold down the fort, Hawkeyes," he'd said, strolling up the aisle.

It wasn't until after he had learned of Janice's impending divorce settlement that he remarked to us kids that in addition to having already gotten her *business* he might also now get some business. My brother and I overheard a phone call between them: she was going to lend him ten thousand dollars. Janice was naïve, way too trusting. We were certain she knew nothing about the drugs.

My father yelled, "What happened to my five-minute warning?"

I told Janice that I had to go and hung up the phone.

I hurried to his room. He'd shaved, combed his hair. I thought the shower might have sobered him some.

"Sorry," I said.

"Your brother home?" he asked.

"Not yet. Is he OK, you think?" He didn't answer. He wasn't paying attention. Or was pretending to not pay attention. He was on his bed struggling to put on a sock that was twisted so the crease popped over his middle toes. "Janice called," I said. "She wants you to call her."

"Did you tell her?"

"Yes, I told her, but she wants you to call her." I waited a few seconds for him to respond. "She said today is no good. She said tomorrow would be great. Maybe this isn't such good idea."

He asked me what I thought about Janice. "Not so pretty as the day we met her, is she? Not like her daughter." He said he could always close his eyes during sex and imagine Reagan instead. "That girl's built for speed." He laughed, slapped his knee. He stared at me until I grinned.

The front door slammed.

My brother charged into the bedroom, ready for a fight.

"Where have you been?" my father asked. "What took you so long?"

"Your friends live on the west side."

My father gnashed his teeth. "I told you to drop them off downtown."

My brother raised his voice. "You told me to take them home."

Instead of firing back my father stopped himself, thought for a moment, trying to recall his exact instructions. His face, gradually turning confused, went blank altogether. He'd lost his train of thought. The pace of the conversation decelerated instantly. You could see the change in my brother's posture too. He just gave up. What was the point?

My father sighed deeply. I turned to him, hopeful for an apology, or even a shred of self-awareness. But it was the second sock—this one inside out. He lifted his legs. I pulled both socks off, put them back on his feet correctly. "Put on a decent shirt," he told my brother. "We're going to meet Janice's mother."

On the way we stopped by the grocery store for flowers. My father was turning in to an open spot when he slammed into the car parked next to us. He reversed, the cars scraped apart. He realigned and pulled in straight.

"Be right back," he said.

My brother and I got out to survey the damage. There was a huge dent in the center of the other car's door. Our Jeep was fine. My brother jumped into the driver's seat, backed out, pulled up to the yellow curb marked "No Parking" next to the entrance to the grocery store.

"Janice doesn't want us to come over," I said.

"Shut up."

"I'm not joking. I talked to her on the phone."

"What the fuck? I like Janice," my brother said. "I like going to her place."

He liked going there to see Reagan. They were in the same grade, same school, and were always flirting or giggling with each other whenever we hung out at her house.

"Shouldn't we try and stop him?" I asked.

My brother was distracted, engrossed in his own private thoughts.

"What are we going to do?"

Again, he ignored me.

My father came out of the grocery store, sunglasses on, in a burgundy silk shirt and khaki shorts, which he was wearing too high, no doubt to show off what he considered his best feature. He walked into the street, raising his hand to halt traffic. My brother waited, watched him for several seconds, then honked.

"We're not doing shit," he said finally. "Fuck him."

My father made his way over, hopped into shotgun.

"I thought you were getting flowers," I said.

"Damn it," he said.

He slipped me a twenty.

I came back out a minute later with a bouquet and his change.

We drove south along the Sandias until we veered onto a slender dirt road. Janice's house was a mile or two into the foothills where Albuquerque met wilderness. Mountain lions sometimes dug through her garbage. She had a deck overlooking the city.

When she opened the front door, she asked where our dad was.

He'd dropped us at the driveway, sent us in first to *grease the wheels*. He needed to *take a lap* around the neighborhood before coming in. That wasn't all he was doing, I was sure.

"He'll be back in a minute," my brother said.

"Did you give him my message?" she asked me.

"Yes, I did. I told him."

She shook her head, ushered us inside, closed the door. I half-expected her to lock it.

We followed her upstairs to the kitchen, where an older woman was struggling to open a bottle of wine. She looked like Janice, short and frumpy, with closely cropped hair parted neatly down the side and combed over like a man's. Janice introduced her mother as Patricia, who told us to call her Pat. She then introduced us as the children of her "new financial advisor." At that we understood that she had not wanted us to come over because of her recent divorce, all this being too soon.

My brother broke the ice, asked Pat about her stay in Albuquerque. I popped the cork, poured two glasses. My father was taking his time, and the more he took, the more my breath came back to me. I'd been holding it all afternoon. My brother seemed unaffected by the awkwardness. He was enjoying the tension, relishing what was to come. I felt sorry for Janice. For myself too, but still this was her home, her family, and we'd been thrown at them. She kept checking her watch, holding a smile, attempting to appear hospitable. She must have maintained the same forced expression for a half hour before my father finally crept around the corner, roared as if on stage, "So, this is the mother?" Pat swung around right into a hug. "I've heard so much about you," he lied, pretending to be closer to Janice than he was.

Pat staggered back, flowers now in her hands. She turned to her daughter. "Who is this handsome man with such polite children?"

"I told you, Mother."

"Yes, I know, your new financial advisor." Pat winked at my father. "Won't you stay for a glass of wine?"

"No," Janice said. "You'll be late for your other appointment, won't you? Didn't you say you had somewhere else to be?" Janice went to her purse, pulled out a bank

envelope, handed it to my father. "Thank you for stopping by."

My father pulled a money order from the envelope,
examined it. In reference to business he always said, *Get
a yes and get out.* He'd gotten the money. It was time to
go. We still might have been able to make it to the bank
before it closed. But I could tell by the look on his face
that we weren't going anywhere. He was stunned and
insulted, thinking that if one of them had the right to be
embarrassed it was him for dating her.

"A glass of wine would be lovely," he said.

In the living room my father sat next to Pat. Janice positioned herself close to the two of them. More than
once she tried to trap my father with eye contact. He
avoided looking in her direction, ignored her completely.
He'd scooted up to the edge of the couch, kept himself
angled toward Pat. Whatever he'd done out in the Jeep
had helped him flip a switch. If anything now he was
too loud, too energetic, his lungs drawing more than his
share of oxygen. Janice's reservations about our meeting
her mother were swallowed up by his big baying laugh.

From nowhere my brother suddenly gasped.

My father turned to him with a sharp aggressive glare.

It was a warning: this is my show—don't interrupt.

Everyone went silent until my brother apologized.

Seconds later he nudged me to look at our dad. At first glance, though, I couldn't find anything out of the ordinary. Up and down, nothing seemed different about my father. I turned to ask my brother for a hint and saw out of the corner of my eye what he'd wanted to show me. At the edge of the couch, his shorts having rolled back, my dad's balls were dangling against the sofa. I turned away, then glanced again, a little longer this time. I had to stop myself from gawking. I bit my fist to keep from cracking up. My father was clueless. He had no idea. He was a primate masquerading as a human, an ape sipping from a stemmed glass. My brother must have thought so too because when our dad scratched his head, we both burst into laughter.

"Shut. Up!" my father yelled. He held his scowl this time.

Quiet filled the room.

Even Pat looked uncomfortable.

Janice started but then stopped.

No one knew what to say next.

My father apologized to Pat for us and asked, "What were you saying, dear?"

My brother flashed me a wry smile. I eyed Janice. She was too transfixed by her dilemma to notice anything. Plus she didn't have the best angle to see. She turned to the doorway as Reagan walked into the room. Reagan went to kiss her grandmother on the cheek, then said hello to everyone else. She gave my brother a sweet smile.

"What's new, babe?" my father asked her.

She did not answer immediately. She hadn't heard him. She was making her way to my brother, who was eagerly waving her over. When she sat down, I saw him tip his head to clue her in, direct her eyes to our dad's shorts. She turned to my father, studied him, his testicles now hanging prominently over the seam of the seat cushion. My mood changed in an instant. I felt myself come alive in Reagan's silence. I wanted her to see. I wanted my father humiliated. I hated him at this moment. But instead she turned to my brother and shrugged. A flood of anger washed over me. My father would get away with this for a lifetime—the arrogance, the self-regard, the lack of consequences.

"Well?" my father said.

"Sorry, what?" Reagan said, facing him again.

"How have you . . ."

She shrieked. She covered her mouth, drew her legs up to her chest. She looked at my brother, then at me, her eyes growing wider. She knew. I was overjoyed. The thrill of hatred consumed me again, and we all turned to my father together, howling as if on cue.

"What's so funny?" he said, his anger rising.

"What's gotten into you rotten children?" Pat said.

"Stop it. All of you!" my father roared. "Stop it, now!"

Janice tried to intervene. She asked my father for a word in the other room.

Instead he stood, became more threatening. The cuffs of his shorts dropped. His balls back in their place made us laugh even louder. "What the fuck is so funny?" he screamed. "Stop fucking laughing!"

His wineglass shattered in his hand.

"In the kitchen, now!" Janice yelled.

Her raised voice stopped us all cold. It was so unnatural, so unlike her. She commanded the room, our laughter dying down quickly, her finger directing my father to the doorway. He looked at his hand. It was bleeding onto the carpet. He put it in his pocket, mumbled an apology to the floor. "Please excuse me," he said. He followed Janice into the next room, that dumb hangdog look on his face.

Out on the porch I watched the city swell before the sunset. Isolated rainstorms looked like pencil scratches in the distance. Inside, Reagan and my brother set the table. Janice and her mother prepared dinner. After they'd spoken in the kitchen, my father left the house, drove off. He probably went straight to the bank. I could have guessed the line he'd used on Janice to explain his behavior—single dad, struggling business, sleep deprived from stress. He'd probably even convinced her to babysit us for the night. Either way it didn't matter. I wasn't mad at him any longer. The more I replayed the scene in my head, the less I enjoyed it. My instinct earlier in the day had been to protect him from himself, then, after, I'd wanted his complete loss of face. Now I heard the echo of cruel laughter. But mostly I was just relieved that I hadn't had to leave with him.

My thoughts drifted to Kansas. It was an hour later there, an hour closer to sleep, to forgetting about everything for eight hours by just closing my eyes. My mother would sometimes scratch my back before bed, and I'd get a strange tickling sensation that started near my tailbone and would stiffen my muscles all the way to my neck. It was innocent, but I was embarrassed because I was too old, and besides, I was on my father's team, and I'd ask her to stop and she would. I stayed out on Janice's porch, calm and alone, until the last light of day faded from the sky, and Albuquerque lit up like a thousand little campfires, and my brother came out to tell me that it was time to eat.

SEVEN

More than a month had passed. We hadn't seen our dad. Not before school, already high, shuffling around the apartment with his slow languid ways. Not after either, sitting down to his desk, pretending to sort papers, pick up the phone, work a pen. Since Janice had given him the check, our only proof of life was at night. Soon after we closed our door to go to bed, we'd listen for his door to creak open, for his padded steps out into the living room, for the low hum of the speakers as he turned on the stereo. He played the same CD on repeat every night until morning, the one he bought from the Spanish guitarist when we'd just moved here.

At first we weren't alarmed. But when one week turned to two, my brother had to cash his own paycheck for groceries, gas, school supplies. After the third week we finally knocked on my father's door. We told him about the bills, the rent, the business line—the red message light on the answering machine had been flashing all this time. He didn't answer. "What do you want us to do?" my brother asked. "Tell us, Dad, what should we do?" I dropped to my knees, peered through the crack at the foot of his door. A lank shadow crept across the carpet. "Dad?" I said. The shadow kept creeping, deliberate as a sloth. The next morning a blank check was sitting on the kitchen table, and the red message light was dark—though it was blinking again when we got home from school.

Tonight, headlights from the street outside our window moved across the wall of our bedroom.

"We need to call Mom," my brother said.

He'd been trying to convince me for a week.

"No," I said. "No way. We'll be fine."

"We won't be fine," he said. "None of this is fine. You know I'm right. Admit it."

I beat back his persuasiveness with thoughts of my dad. I imagined him staring out the window to the park, the only light in the room the ember of his cigar, reflecting sadly on the things he'd done, people he'd lost, pushed away. Sometimes in my mind I was my father. After all, weren't he and I totally beyond forgiveness? Weren't we the two who had betrayed my mother the worst? And what made my brother think she could help? She'd never stood up to our dad before. Why would she now?

"Not yet," I said. "He'll bounce back. You'll see."

"How much longer do we have to wait?"

I begged him for more time.

He went quiet. Then he scooted down in bed, his silence a sign of assent.

"What the hell is she going to do for us anyway?" I said.

Before falling asleep we heard his door open, footsteps, a woman's voice, the opening and closing of the front door, the dead bolt flick, the chain lock latch. My brother was already looking out the window, whispering to me the description of a woman we did not recognize walk out to the street and disappear into the night. We kept our eyes on the parking lot. Nothing came back out of the darkness. The music began a moment later.

There was a soft knock on our bedroom door a week later. She said my name. She'd been back most nights. I'd learned to recognize her voice—the lack of lilt due to the drugs. I climbed from bed, cracked the door, careful not to wake my brother.

"Be my eyes," she whispered.

I nodded, turned to the window.

"Wait," she said. "What does it mean? Be my eyes?"

"It means play lookout," I told her, my voice hushed. "Keep an eye on the street."

"What are you looking for?"

"Anything suspicious," I said.

"Oh?" she said, excited. "Why don't I be lookout at the back window?"

My eyes finally adjusted to the darkness. Her eyes were big and encouraging. Her lips thin, puckered. She wanted me to think she was pretty. She was asking for some sort of consent, as if she needed my approval in order to get high with my father. As if she needed my approval in spite of getting high with him.

I stepped back, said OK.

Out the window the street was empty, all quiet. I could hear my brother breathing in his sleep. I watched him. When we were young our parents gave us dream catchers as gifts from a trip they'd taken to the Southwest. My brother, unsure how they worked, slept with his on his face that first night. He'd slipped his tiny nose through the web, balanced a feather on the tip of his chin. My mother probably still had the photo of it.

I tiptoed to the living room. The CD played softly from the stereo. Light leaked out from beneath my father's door. His friend stood before the window, cigarette smoke twisting up from the ashtray. "You see anything?" she asked.

I shook my head.

"Have you ever seen anything?"

I shrugged.

"Maybe tonight."

"Maybe."

I lingered for a moment, wanted to know if my father had said anything else. Maybe she'd forgotten to relay a message. Instead I asked her if he was OK. I said we hadn't seen him in a while. "I'm worried about him," I told her.

She turned to me, the night illuminating half her face.

"His boys is all he talks about," she said.

Though the one in the ashtray still burned, she lit another cigarette. She turned to the window again, resumed her role as lookout, waited for me to go back to bed. I knew she didn't plan to keep watch after I left. The force inside my father's bedroom was calling her to return. She would not stay in orbit much longer.

At the grocery store I strolled the movie rentals, the frozen food aisle, the dairy section. I saw my brother's hands behind the glass, stocking cartons of milk. I opened the door, grabbed his wrist.

"I'll give you something to milk," I said.

"Motherfucker, you scared me," he said. "That's going to cost you."

"Bullshit."

"Three," he said. "My choice."

"No. Shoulder only."

"My choice."

After his shift my brother socked me in the thigh out-side the store.

I limped away a few feet. "I said shoulder only."

He smiled, pulled out a fistful of bills. He'd just cashed his check. He looked to the sky. "Come on, we're going to miss it."

The sun had nearly set when the balloon glow began. Hundreds of hot-air balloons firing up their flames be-fore the dying day. One by one, the sky grown dark, they lifted, weightless and radiant. At highway speeds these balloons would be in flight through the night and for sev-eral days after, until a winner, having landed somewhere in Minnesota or thereabouts, had flown farthest from the fairgrounds. My brother pointed at one, way high. As boys we used to lie in our backyard, stare up at the sky together. My brother would locate a cloud, usually a solitary one, and with the force of our gaze we would make it stop drifting. The cloud motionless, we felt the earth rotating beneath us. I got that same giddy feeling in my stomach now—part terror, part anticipation—that at any moment we might slip from the face of the planet.

The balloons out of sight, the fiesta began. We ate hot dogs and funnel cake, drank pop. We stood in the back of the crowd away from the stage as a band started to play. The whole time, though, I sensed our dad watching us. It was my guilt over spending too much. I felt bad for wasting money. My brother saw me withdrawing into my thoughts.

"Don't," he said. "This is our revenge."

I nodded.

He slapped me on the back. "Come on."

I followed him to the carnival games.

At each new booth he fanned out more cash.

On our return to the Jeep a man walked out from between two cars, cut us off in the parking lot. My heart raced, senses sharpened. Off in the distance there was the sound of laughter, music, a loud crack in the sky. My brother moved to shield me. But his body suddenly arched like a parenthesis, slammed onto the ground. I was also tackled from behind. My face skidded across the gravel. The man on top of me turned me over, emptied my pockets. There was nothing in them. He snarled, pushed my raw cheek down into the road. When the three of them ran away, I rolled to my side. My brother was hunched over on his knees, holding his stomach, appearing to protect a wound.

I asked him if he was hurt.

He grunted.

"Are you hurt?" I yelled.

He gasped for air, shook his head.

"Wind knocked out of you?"

He nodded.

I lay back down on the ground.

Once he caught his breath, we helped each other to our feet. By the light of the fireworks he double-checked his pockets. The money was all gone.

He used his shirt to wipe my face.

"You're all scraped up," he said.

"Your lip's split."

He tongued his lip.

"Mom should see us now," he said.

He mentioned her like she'd be waiting for us at home.

"Why's that?" I asked.

"She always said: God help the day one of you comes home with a black eye and the other one doesn't."

I went next, "You both come home with black eyes or don't come home at all."

We continued impersonating her the whole drive back, even though laughing made my face hurt, his ribs ache. I felt close to my brother, which I was thankful for, and as we pulled into the complex, the lights in the apartment off, I felt thankful too for my father's absence.

She knocked that night as well. My brother woke before me. He answered the door. "Be my eyes," I heard her say. She used my name again. He nodded. She walked away. He went to the window. I'd never seen my brother play lookout. I didn't even know he knew about it. I rolled over to watch him. From the streetlight the edges of his profile glowed.

"How long has it been you?" he asked. "I didn't know he still did this."

I sat up in bed. "Are you jealous?"

"I thought he'd stopped is all."

He turned to me, but his eyes suddenly darted to the door.

It was the woman, staring silently, looking at one of us and then the other, a confused or curious expression on her face. Then she turned, went to the kitchen. When she came back into our room she placed melting ice cubes in our hands. She waited eagerly for us to put them to our wounds. She stood next to my brother, gazed out the window. He soaked up the attention. He asked her how our dad was. "We need him back," he said. "Tell him we can't do this alone." By the way his voice broke, it was obvious that he was speaking for himself, for both of us, not just for me. I'd thought he'd given up on our father.

"OK," she hushed him, "I'll tell him. Go to sleep now."

The next morning the apartment smelled of lemon and cleaning supplies. She'd used bleach on the table, which had stripped the stain. Spot-cleaned the carpet with it too. Wood polish now fogged the windows, the wall hangings. But for these few details the place was immaculate. On the kitchen counter were two brown paper bags, filled up, stapled shut. She'd even packed us lunch.

The day we finally saw him, I returned from school to find my brother sitting on the ground outside the apartment. He said they were fighting inside. "About what?" I asked. He didn't know. "About us?" He shrugged. I heard their raised voices. I thought she might have been standing up to my father, reminding him that he had kids.

I knocked on the door, said it was us, his sons.

The blinds rustled. The window rose.

"Boys?" my father said.

"Dad?"

"Come back later."

The door flew open.

"You fucking thief," she yelled. She rushed out, ran wildly into the parking lot, a lunatic escaping in daylight. She turned back, flipped us the middle finger. "Fuck you, asshole. Fuck all three of you motherfuckers."

My father ushered us in hurriedly, closed the door.

I didn't recognize him. His lips were blistered, cracked. He'd thinned—his mustache too big for his face. His pants didn't fit him anymore. He had to hold them up by the waistband. The frays of his cuffs dragged across the carpet like uprooted plants. His uneasy energy frightened us both, especially with how weak he appeared, how slow moving. He was an electronic device running out of charge. We kept our distance.

The phone started ringing.

"Battle stations," he cried.

"What happened?" my brother asked. "What's going on?"

"That bitch called the cops." His hands had begun to shake. "You have to bail me out. You can't leave me in jail. You hear me?"

"Why'd she call the cops?" my brother asked.

"You hear me? You can't leave me in there. That'd be like killing me. My death would be on your hands."

"What was the argument about? You stole something from her," I said.

"She thought it was all hers." He said it like a child. "Greedy bitch."

"What did she tell the cops?" my brother asked.

"Nothing. I hung up the phone before she could say anything."

"Is that them calling now?" my brother said.

The phone stopped ringing.

"Battle stations," he cried again.

My brother secured the apartment. He tightened the blinds, locked the windows, bolted the door. I played lookout from our bedroom. My father was in his room straightening up. A police cruiser rolled to a stop outside our building. I ran to tell them.

In a panic we all crammed together under his desk, my father in the middle.

The plan was: keep quiet and wait for the cop to leave.

The officer knocked, announced himself.

He knocked a second time, harder.

We saw his shadow behind the blinds of the window next to the front door, his hands cupped over his brow. When his shadow disappeared, I leaned out from beneath the desk to see it arrive at our bedroom window. I pointed to show my brother. My father's head was buried between his legs. The officer stood there awhile, then was gone again. Moments later we heard him walking on the rocks behind the apartment. He jumped the railing to the back porch. He was right over us. My father shook horribly, his muscles convulsing. I put my arms around him, squeezed as hard as I could to settle his nerves. The officer tested the windows above the desk. They both stuck. He had the same result with the glass porch door. My eyes met my brother's, and while mine expressed gratitude to him for locking up, for being reliable and doing his job well, I was devastated to find his full of disgust for the scene of me cradling our dad.

At the front door the cop knocked a last time. Then it sounded like he tried the neighbors. There was no answer there either. The sun was setting, the officer's shadow no longer detectable in the window, and though we didn't know if he'd left or not, we remained quiet beneath the desk until darkness was complete and my father had stopped shaking.

There was no music that night. We'd put our dad to bed. In our room I searched for a way to persuade my brother not to contact our mom. The closer he came to calling her, the more certain I was that I never wanted to live with her again. It wasn't just that she was unreliable, but that in my most private thoughts I feared her forgiveness. The ease with which she'd brush it all under the rug, blame my father, pretend that it was not my fault at all. It couldn't be real. It wouldn't last. She'd never be able to hold back her disappointment in me. And what about our father? We would have to leave him behind, betray him, too.

"What about Dad?" I asked. "He wouldn't survive. He'd die without us."

My brother had made his decision. He'd broken from the boys.

"Let him," he said. "I don't care anymore."

"You can't call her," I said. "She won't forgive us."

"Yes, she will."

"She won't forgive me."

"I bet she already has."

My eyes burned with anger. I didn't know who to blame. I went out to the living room to sleep on the couch.

All night I dreamed in short clips. There was one: a scene from a trip I'd taken with my father to Colorado years ago, except we'd switched roles. I stood watching as he explored a great plateau on the other side of a mountain bridge. It was daytime, autumn. The aspens were yellow and orange, and their wispy leaves flickered in the wind. My father had begun to walk back to me but had veered off the path, away from the bridge, toward a cliff. And at the point when in real life my father had yelled out, redirected me away from the edge, in the dream I was muted, immobile, my expression indifferent, while inside I screamed and flailed and wept—a great wind that would not blow.

EIGHT

My father threw open our bedroom door, began to pace about in his underwear like a prisoner obsessed with his own innocence, ranting, "Traitor! Traitor! Traitor!" I sat up in bed, pulled from sleep by his rage. My brother had already left for school. Today was my day to help my father catch up on office work. He had not yet returned to normal from the months-long binge. The comedown had been prolonged. His hands still shook when he held a glass. He was sensitive to sound. He had no control over the swings of his emotions. He reacted with extremes: weepy or angry—sometimes at the same time.

"My firstborn son," he cried. "Of all the people in the world."

"What happened?" I asked. "What did he do?

"He called the Amalekite."

My father told me that my mother had called back after my brother had left. She said she was taking him to court and taking us kids back. He was going to pay child support.

She even threatened to call the cops. "She's holding us hostage again," he said.

I'd known this day was coming. I'd known it would be messy. But that my brother and father had both spoken to my mother this morning was an actuality I was not prepared for. I felt exposed. She was in our lives again, just like that, as though she'd been here all along.

He stopped pacing, faced me. "How are we going to punish him?"

His question turned real in the silence.

"What do you think?" I asked.

Suddenly he was in my face, screaming, "Why aren't you as mad as me? What's wrong with you? He chose her over us. You want to go live with her too? Is that it? Are you a goddamn traitor too?"

I wiped specks of his saliva from my face. My cheeks turned hot as they always did before I cried. He was asking me to choose between my dad and my brother. I needed him to back away a few feet. I needed space to think. I swung my legs onto the floor, put my head down, pretended to deliberate his question.

My father dropped to his knees. He clutched my bare calves. "Don't give up on me, boy," he said. "Don't you give up on me." He lifted my chin. "How are we going to punish your brother?"

The tears came.

Just a few, and I wiped them away.

"Ground him," I said.

"What else?"

"Spank him."

"We need something more dramatic."

"You could threaten to send him back."

"And if he wants to go back?"

"Let him," I said, finding in this answer a way to also protect my brother. "We don't need him," I lied.

"In medieval times your brother would have been drawn and quartered. You know what that means? The king would have tied his limbs to horses and ripped him to pieces. We need something that'll bring him back in line. Something he'll never forget."

He was looking to me for the answer. I was afraid of what would happen if I did not give him what he wanted, but also of what would happen if I gave him what he was asking.

"We could surprise him when he comes home."

"Could?" he fired back.

"Surprise him," I said.

"Details."

"Hide behind the door."

"Go on."

"Tackle him when he comes through."

He waited for more.

"Tie him up with rope," I said.

"Good," he said. "What else?"

"Then threaten to send him back."

I watched him drift off into his imagination, stage it out, visualize the execution of the plan. All the while he muttered that he loved me, that I was the only person in the world he could trust. I'd gotten off easy, I thought, and maybe so had my brother. But then my father's face turned cruel.

"Treason is a capital offense," he said. "What else?"

"Threaten him with a knife?"

He asked me if that was a question.

"Threaten him with a knife," I said.

All afternoon I waited for my father to come to his senses. When I realized he would not, I tried to make myself angry with my brother. He'd broken the pact—why should I defend him? It didn't work though. I couldn't vilify my brother. But I also refused to warn him. I was too furious with my mother. She knew my father. What did she expect would happen? How could she have been so stupid, so careless? She was the one doing this to my brother. This was her fault. Besides, he would be able to fight us off. These days my brother was about as big as our dad. And I was too young, too weak to be a real factor. Plus I didn't plan to try.

When my brother walked through the door, my father wrapped him up around the waist, pummeled him to the floor. My brother fell hard. He squirmed violently. I jumped on his legs, hugged his ankles, as instructed. My brother had locked his arms beneath his chest. My father warned him to give them up. He drove his knee into the small of my brother's back. My brother groaned, gathered enough momentum to somehow throw my father forward. In the commotion my father's pants had wiggled down. His bare ass was exposed. His face was red from exertion, from humiliation. He jumped back on my brother, yelled at him to stop fighting.

"Fuck you," my brother said.

My dad bit him, twisted free an arm, then pushed my brother's wrist up between his shoulder blades.

"That hurts," my brother cried. He gave up his other arm. "Please. That hurts."

Enough, I wanted to say. We were only supposed to scare him.

My father tied my brother's hands behind his back.

"I'm getting up now," my father told him. "Don't you fucking move."

"I swear," he said.

"Swear what?"

"I swear I won't move."

My father stood, pulled his pants up. He looked to me,

his eyes wild and fevered. He disappeared into the kitchen. My brother turned onto his side to catch his breath. He rolled his hurt shoulder, wiped his running nose on the carpet. He had rope burns on his wrists already. My father had tied them too tight. My brother looked down at me holding his ankles. He was confused and frightened. He didn't understand what I was doing. He bit his lip to make it stop quivering. I loosened my grip, then let go of him completely. We'd hurt him. He'd cried for help. I was horrified by what we'd done.

My father returned to the living room just then. My brother saw the knife in his hand. He scurried backwards across the carpet until he hit the wall. My father stepped slowly toward him. With each sentence his voice rose. "This is your fault," he said. "You called the Amalekite. You turned your back on us. You forced our hand. You have something you want to say to us now, don't you? Tell us! Tell us you're sorry! Tell us you gave us no choice. That we are right to do this to you. That you deserve it. You're a coward and a traitor! Now put your tail between your legs and show us your ass." My father crouched, got in my brother's face. He pointed at me. "Better yet, look at your brother over there. He's the one whose heart you broke. This was all his idea. Even he knew you had to be brought back in line. Look at him. Tell him you're sorry. Admit to him that you're no different from your cunt mother!"

My brother's eyes, no longer filled with fear, now beamed with exhilaration. They were big and boyish too. In them I saw us both back in Kansas, years younger, racing each other home from school on our bikes. We drop our bags at the back porch, run off into the woods to play. We hide, one of us challenging the other to come find him. Before the broken dishes and private investigators he hunts for me amid trees just wider than we are, and I keep a hand over my mouth to not let laughter betray my position. We were happy. He was all I had left of that time. I jumped up, leaped across the room, threw myself onto my brother. I shielded him and begged his forgiveness.

I was pulled from my brother's body by my hair. My father's backhand sent me staggering across the room. I crashed into the coffee table. Glass shattered around me, which seemed to send my father into a fury. He screamed that this was exactly what our mother had meant to do— divide and conquer. How had we forgotten? Why were our memories so short? Why weren't we on his side? He worked himself into such a state that he drove his fist into my brother's face. He flipped him onto his stomach, lifted him by the rope around his wrists, dragged him facedown across the carpet. My brother writhed in pain. His shoulders looked like they might rip from their sockets. My father threw him onto the couch, put the knife right up to his throat.

"Tell me you're sorry. Tell me you'll never do it again," he said. "You want this to stop? I need something from you first. I want your fucking word."

My brother blubbered incoherently.

My father yelled at him to stop crying, apologize, get it over with. "You have the power to end this. Just promise you'll never do it again. Just say the words."

My brother's breath was spastic. He tried to quiet himself. Then to say something. He hardly mustered, "I, I, I, I, I . . ."

"If you can't speak, shut up," my father said. "Just shut the fuck up."

He threw the knife to his side, put his hand over my brother's mouth.

Wrists still bound, my brother thrashed, struggling to throw my father.

"Why are you fighting me?" my father yelled. "Stop fighting me."

He put his other hand over my brother's mouth to keep control.

"Stop and I'll stop," my father said.

My brother didn't stop. He couldn't breathe. Snot bubbled out of his nose. Spit sounds and muffled screams came from his mouth. He shook his head side-to-side. He thrust his hips, kicked his legs. My father kept his hands pressed down. I watched all this paralyzed by fear. "I'll kill you," my father said, his voice cracking. "Stop or I'll kill you." Then my father's body suddenly shuddered. He fell on top of my brother, wrapped his arms around his son. My brother jolted up, gasped for air, shoved him off the couch. There on the floor our dad began to sob, and a look came over his face like he didn't know who he was, or where.

That night, after my brother and I had cleaned up and dragged the coffee table to the Dumpster, my father called him into his room. I listened outside the door as he told my brother that he should never have contacted our mom. That we'd felt betrayed and did not know what else to do. "I would never hurt you," my father said. "We only meant to scare you. Please forgive me. Do you forgive me?" Then he said, "Thank you. I forgive you, too. Can I have a hug?" The bed squeaked as my father scooted closer, I guessed, because a moment later he said, "Put your arms around me, son."

I stepped outside to the park.

Overhead the moon was hidden. Clouds were backlit at their feathery edges. A strong wind from the east, from the Sandias, swept over the grass. I winced at the thought of today. My father turned us against each other—it was his method of control. And I'd fallen for it again. Any remorse I had for the Polaroids now felt false. I had let down my brother, just as I had my mom. I was so disappointed in myself, and I swore then that I would never again choose my father. I never again wanted to harm anyone I loved. I was on my brother's side now. He was my brother for life. I'd been lucky today that he had not been more seriously hurt.

A flock of birds came to rest on a nearby piñon tree, populating its limbs like leaves. And though I could hardly see them, hardly hear them, I was happy for their quiet company and hoped they would not leave me soon.

NINE

We were dropping our dad off at the airport. The *big account* was gone. The call came a week back. He'd been asked to return to Kansas to tie up loose ends. Once he was out of town, my brother and I were leaving New Mexico for good, forever. My brother had secretly kept contact with our mom over the past few weeks. The bus tickets were already bought. He'd told me the plan a few nights ago in bed.

"Does she know about the knife?" I'd asked him.

He nodded.

"The whole story?"

"Yes," he said.

"Good," I said.

The war was one of information. The more she knew, the better.

It was morning, cold. The sun had not yet crested the Sandias. The earth was still dark. My father drove. He was dressed for a different kind of December. He reached behind his chair to tickle my brother in the backseat. My brother shied from contact. Neither of us had spoken to him in weeks. We avoided him as much as possible. He seemed to understand why. Or he at least seemed confident that we'd eventually come back around.

"You hear a fat lady?" my father said. "I don't hear a fat lady. Means we haven't lost yet. There's still time to make you boys proud of your papa."

He pulled into Albuquerque International Airport, parked in front of the departure terminal. My brother switched to the driver's seat. I met my father at the trunk. I'd imagined this moment for the past few days, trying to think up some small gesture he wouldn't be able to decode. I didn't know when I would see him again. I'd decided that helping him with his bag would be kind of like a good-bye. I grabbed his roller, handed it to him. His face turned shy and full of gratitude. He smiled, moved to hug me. But then he stopped, went still, froze completely. I saw him fill up with worry. Had he figured it out? Was my gesture that obvious? I followed his eyes to a police officer who had come out the sliding doors and struck up conversation with a skycap.

My father threw his bag back in the trunk, told me to get in the car.

He jumped into the backseat. I took shotgun.

"Drive," he said.

We took a lap around the airport.

At the economy lot he directed my brother to pull in, park.

The ignition off, we heard my father's long slow breaths.

"I should just shut up," he said. "I haven't worked this stuff out yet in my head." He took a moment, started again. "As you get older, if you're paying attention, you learn a lot about yourself. It's easier, you get it? Behavioral trends become kind of obvious over the course of a lifetime. There's more data to interpret." He thought for a moment, planned what to say next. "Over the past few weeks I've learned that I engage in two kinds of activities: self-improvement and self-destruction. The day the police showed up, I realized that my greatest fear, my worst fucking nightmare, is going to jail. I can't do it. Not ever. I got so fucking close that time, and I've found myself wondering ever since: What happened to me? How did I lose control? I'm telling you boys the truth now when I say that I haven't used since that day." His tone dropped to a tremble. "I'm going to fix this. I'm going to win back the big account. I'm going to make you proud of me. I wasn't always like this, remember? The drive down here I was a kid again, wasn't I?"

My father's sadness was drawing me in. I looked to my brother to gauge his reaction. He kept his mouth shut, eyes forward. I followed his lead.

"I have cocaine on me now," my father said.

My brother got out of the Jeep, slammed the door, sat down on the curb.

After an awkward silence my father asked me if he could talk out loud for a while. "You don't need to respond," he said. "You don't have to say anything. Please just don't get out of the car. I think I need someone to listen to me for a minute. I can explain. I don't want to use the stuff. I just wanted to travel with it. It makes me feel safe knowing that it's there. I should get rid of it, I know. I need to get rid of it. Get rid of it," he implored himself. "I'll just blow it all in the bathroom is what I'll do. I'll flush it down the toilet, OK?" Then his voice broke as he asked: "Your brother still loves me, doesn't he?"

For so long it had been my job to comfort my father. He was asking for the same generosity I'd given him a thousand times before. In fact one kind word from me would have made us both feel better. But that was over now. I opened the door, sat down next to my brother on the curb.

My father took his time getting out of the Jeep. He walked slowly to the trunk, grabbed his bag. He approached us, invited us inside the terminal. He had some time to kill before his flight and thought we all could sit at the bar, have a bite, play hooky from school. He needed his boys near him. We were his strength, he told us. "We could just watch TV, if you don't want to talk."

My brother and I remained quiet.

The silence grew comfortable and still.

My father rolled his bag to the exit, took the stairs.

That afternoon, our bags packed and sitting by the door, the phone rang. My brother picked it up. It was our mom. We'd been waiting to hear from her. My brother wrote down the specifics: times, addresses, confirmation codes. We were leaving first thing in the morning. When they were finished talking, my brother tried handing me the receiver.

I blurted out that I'd rather speak to her in person.

She heard me. I heard her say she loved me.

There was strength in her voice. I'd remembered it differently.

My brother said good-bye, hung up.

He went straight to the freezer, took out the peppermint schnapps, poured two glasses. He knocked his back all the way. I followed his lead. The booze stifled my breath at first, closed up my throat, but then it got easier to breathe. He poured us another. I went to the window, opened the blinds to let in the day.

After the second drink my brother pulled his pants down, started rubbing himself against the couch. He scooted across the carpet like a dog with an ass itch. I pissed in the dishwasher. We put on my father's CD of the Spanish guitarist and walked around like zombies, bumping into walls. Only a few minutes before, when my brother was speaking to our mom, I had been crippled by the fear of siding against our dad. I was paranoid that this was all a ruse, that he was somehow watching us, that he was behind his bedroom door, ear to the receiver, ready to run out, call me a traitor. He'd say that I'd always been on my mother's team. He'd tell me that no one in our family trusted me. He'd want me to know that I had orphaned myself. Now the butterflies stirring up a fit in my stomach came to rest, and I stopped asking the questions I only just realized I'd been repeating to myself my entire life: What does my father need from me right now? What am I doing wrong? How can I make him happy? In his absence the apartment felt enormous. We could do anything, go anywhere. Even so, we needed a third drink to try his bedroom door.

"I'll take the dresser," my brother said. "You get the closet."

In the closet the smell of his cologne lingered. I checked a jacket pocket, sniffed a collar, fanned ties on his tie rack. After a step back I took in his suits and shirts and slacks. There was a shoe box on the top shelf. I called my brother over to grab it. We sat down on the bed to examine the contents.

We were surprised to find the box filled with mementos—photos, keepsakes, letters—mostly of our mom. Near the top was a finger-worn postcard with the red sun symbol and yellow field of the New Mexican flag. My mother's handwriting was on the other side. It was from the trip they'd taken out here years back. It was addressed to our house in Kansas, postmarked in Santa Fe. She must have mailed it to him secretly.

We read to ourselves.

Sweetness and Light, she called him. *Whenever we fight like two nights ago in Oklahoma City, I always think about how precious our time is together. I wonder though where the tender moments are? Why aren't there more? Its not just that I feel sad when we don't get along, but that I feel like we are throwing away something special. I love you so much, but you scare me sometimes. When you left me at the motel, I waited up for you all night. The whole time I felt so ashamed. I hated myself because it wasn't until the door slammed shut that I remembered to love you better. I want us to feel that way always. I want us to remember to be kind to each other. We always come back together stronger than ever, but lets make a promise for our new life in New Mexico. Lets promise to fight less and love more.* She signed off with *Always* and her name.

"We were all moving down here together at one point?" I asked my brother. "Why would he keep this stuff?" He ignored my questions. "Do you really think Mom will come through?"

"Stop," he yelled. "Just fucking stop talking."

He closed the box, put it away. I followed him into the living room. He punched the power button on the stereo. The music went off. He poured us another drink. We sipped our glasses. After a moment he said, "She's on our side now."

We looked around the room for our next activity.

My eyes stopped at *The Spirit* resting on the fireplace mantle. I'd sometimes come home from school to find my dad sitting on the couch, staring at the elegant alabaster sculpture. Now, shafts of light from the window brought her to life, made her dress glint, nose wrinkle, mouth move to whisper some secret I'd once believed my father had long understood.

"Her." I pointed.

"What about her?"

"Let's bury the bitch," I said.

He laughed. "Where?"

"The park?"

"No shovel."

"A hammer, then."

In the park, though, we were too drunk for that. We dropped the sculpture on the grass, sat down next to her. Night was near. We scooted close to each other. My brother put his hand on my knee, and I finally felt the gravity of the moment: We were leaving. It was happening. My heart sank from the weight of the realization that I didn't think I could ever see my father again. It would be too difficult to explain why we left, too easy for him to manipulate me. His logic was always so simple—I was giving up on him. But I also felt exhilarated to run, to never return. I pictured my brother and me fleeing on a bus—our eyes glued to the window as winter arrived and the skyline slowly straightened—and I knew we were making the right decision.

"Come on," my brother said. "It's freezing. Let's go back inside."

We left *The Spirit* out in the park, facing east.

The snow had dumped while we slept. The interstate was plowed, visibility good but for brief moments when overnight buildup swept from the tops of trailers, poured over the bus's windshield. New Mexico's eastern plain was blank, featureless. We could not measure our progress in mile markers or tanks of gas or changes in the land as we had done on the drive down. I traced power lines instead. The wind sometimes lashed the bus over the lane line. We stopped in Amarillo for lunch in the early afternoon.

Inside the bus terminal my brother called our mom from the pay phone.

I went to the bathroom, checked out the snacks in the vending machine. On my way back across the lounge I saw my brother's shoulders hunched in anger. His hand covered his mouth as he whispered furiously into the phone. He saw me, waved me to hustle over.

He shared the phone so I could listen.

"Honey," my mother said, "you need to trust me."

"No," my brother said. "Fuck that."

"This is what's best for us," she said.

I asked him what was going on.

"Dad's been with her since this morning," he said.

"Is that your brother?" she asked. "Let me talk to him."

He handed me the phone.

"Honey, you there?"

"Yes," I said.

"He showed up on my doorstep early this morning. We've been talking since sunrise. He's told me everything. Everything your brother told me and more. He's been a monster. He knows it. But he also knows how brave you boys have been. He's made terrible mistakes, unforgivable, but he wants to try and start over. He wants to make it right. He says he'll move you all back here. It was his idea. He had no idea that you were already on your way."

"He knows where we are right now?" I said. "You told him?"

"He's not angry. He understands."

"I want my family back," I heard him say in the background.

"He wants his family back," she said.

"Tell him our deal," he said.

"Did you know your dad has been clean for over a month? But he needs extra help. You boys are going to stay with me until he's well. He'll put it in writing that I get full custody if he doesn't stay sober for a year. He's even going to lift the restraining order. Doesn't that sound like he's ready to change?" She explained that now we needed to grab a bus back to Albuquerque. We had to complete the last two weeks of class before Christmas. Over winter break we'd *pack up and ship out*, a phrase of my father's she was obviously repeating. "How's that sound? Better, right? This way we do it out in the open. Legal."

My brother, listening in, had heard enough. He threw his hands up and went outside. I watched him through the window pace in the snow. He was pissed at her. I was too. She didn't understand how exposed we were. How exposed she had just made us. And now she wanted us to go back? But then again our parents were talking right now. They were in the same room. If my father kept his word, what was a few more weeks?

"You believe him?" I asked her.

"I see the man I married," she said.

Outside I spoke to my brother.

"I'll do whatever you want," I told him. "Tell me what you want to do. We can stay on this bus all the way to Kansas. We can go steal the Jeep and run. Just drive."

"We'd get caught," he said.

"We'd have a few days of freedom at least. What are our other options?"

"We don't have any."

"Are they going to get back together?"

"It's what they both deserve," he said.

He went inside, called our mom. We were on the next bus back.

By the time we got to Albuquerque it was dark. We cleared the snow off the Jeep with our hands, drove home from the bus station. Back at the apartment the red message light on the answering machine was blinking. My brother hit the button. Our parents had left us a voice mail. They were yelling over the noise in the background. They were out celebrating. My father had won back the *big account*. "Good things happen when you make good choices," my mother said. He called her "Sweetness and Light." They'd decided he would stay in Kansas through the weekend.

We didn't hear from them for a few days. The snow had stopped. Still, school was canceled. We stayed inside mostly. My brother kept to himself. From the window I thought I could see the head of *The Spirit* poking through the snow cover. I went out to look for it on Saturday. It was nowhere to be found.

Sunday morning the phone rang. My brother muted the TV.

My mother came over the answering machine. She asked for me.

In Amarillo I had been relieved that our first conversation in so long had been about something pressing, immediate. By now I'd grown eager to speak to her for real. I wanted the reconciliation over with. I was sure it was why she was calling.

My brother asked me what I was waiting for.

I answered the phone.

"Honey," she said. "Can you talk?"

I jumped right in, told her about the day I lied to the social worker. I wanted her to understand the pressure I'd felt to perform for my father. She hushed me. She was crying already. So was I.

"It's not your fault. None of this is your fault."

"Yes it is," I said. "Please don't lie to me."

"Let's just start over. We'll wipe the slate clean. Past is past."

"You don't have to do that. I don't think it's even possible."

"I don't know how to do this. What should I say? I want my boys back."

"Dad too?" I asked.

"I don't know," she said. "Maybe."

"Is he listening?"

"He's still asleep."

"We're afraid of him."

"I know. So am I." There was a long silence before she spoke again. "When you were in preschool, you and your brother were playing around one morning, jumping on the bed. I was downstairs in the kitchen, and I heard a thud and ran upstairs as fast as I could and found you huddled up on the floor, holding your shoulder. I wanted to take you to the doctor right away, but your dad said no. He thought you were being dramatic. Well, stupid as I was, I listened to him. I took you to school and walked you to your classroom and sat you down in your chair, and when I came back at the end of the day to pick you up, you hadn't moved an inch. You were still sitting in the same seat where I left you, and in the same position too. My poor baby! Your collarbone was broken. I nearly screamed at your teacher. I wanted to kill your dad. You were so stiff when I helped you up out of that chair, but you barely made a noise. A part of me, a secret part, was proud of your tolerance for pain. That's my child, I thought. He has my strength. But when we were leaving the hospital,

I asked you why you didn't say anything to your teacher. I wanted to know why you decided to put yourself through something so awful. 'That's how you stay one of the boys,' you told me. My heart broke in that moment. That's the way I've remembered you over the past two years, the memory I've kept closest to me." She was done crying, speaking clearly. "I won't put you in a position again where your dad'll hurt you. You don't have to trust him right now. But you can trust me. Deal?"

"Deal," I said.

"I love you so much."

"I love you, too."

She asked to talk to my brother.

They spoke for a short while. He mostly listened. He'd softened some over the past few days. He appeared to be softening even more now. When he was off the phone, he sat down on the couch, turned the volume up, stared at the TV. I could tell he was trying hard to keep a blank expression. A moment later a beautiful smile broke over his face. "Mom's flying out with Dad tomorrow," he said.

My brother picked me up from school the next afternoon. We went straight to the airport, hours early. We walked around, popped into shops, tried to do our homework, looked for distractions. We talked about our old friends back home and our old neighborhood, our old lives, excitedly at first, until the unease that maybe we wouldn't fit in anymore, that maybe we were too different from the versions of ourselves we'd left behind, settled over us. We changed the subject. When their flight was about to land, we took a seat near the baggage claim, kept an eye on the stairs. Last night we'd cleaned the apartment, bought ingredients for dinner, set the table. We hung streamers, made signs. My brother had shaved and had taught me to shave. Our mom was coming down to help us pack. Two weeks here wasn't so long. If all went well, we'd be back in Kansas in no time.

A crowd of passengers started down the stairs. We stood, each of us holding an edge of the poster with her name on it. I could hardly contain my fear, uncertainty, hope. My anticipation warped faces to look like my mother's. I found myself rocking, from one foot to the other, my fists balled. It was a dance, I realized, that she had once shown us. My brother and I, we are watching a baseball game in the living room of her apartment. This is after our parents' separation. It's nighttime, spring. The screens are open. Through the windows we hear the breeze rustle the leaves, and the song of the cicadas, early this year, rising from the field across the street. Our mom walks out of her bedroom in high-waisted pants with well-creased pleats running down to her high heels. She steps as if on stilts until she stands in front of the television. Her silk blouse is tucked in, seems to be melting off her body. She's missed a button. The gap shows her bra, a mole on her breast. That's when we know she's drunk. She's probably taken pills too. Her hair is slicked back, lipstick painted a half inch past her lips. She has on thick blue eyeliner and clumpy mascara. She's begging for our attention.

She balls her fists, pumps them, rocks back and forth, one foot to the other.

"Salt and pepper shaker," she says. "Salt and pepper shaker."

My brother and I are not amused. We don't have much patience for her. She's been sleeping in her room all day. We smile and tell her to get out of the way. She doesn't listen, just goes on repeating that phrase, those movements. She won't stop. We try to resist, but my brother and I eventually lose ourselves to the absurdity. I punch my stomach, the laughter is so deep. He kicks his legs in the air. She feeds off us, keeps dancing. She has no other moves, just pumps her fists faster, quickens her steps, incants, "Salt and pepper shaker. Salt and pepper shaker." Then she loses her footing, falls to a knee. My brother and I jump, run to her, make sure she's OK. She's not hurt. In fact she is laughing so hard she can barely breathe. So are we. After long silent seconds we all gasp for air.

My brother raised our welcome poster higher. A new

wave of people now descended the steps to the baggage claim. I decided to break into her dance, use her line, when I saw her. It would make her feel at home. From nowhere it seemed, my father was halfway down the stairs, hugging the rail, hurrying. I pointed him out. He saw us in the crowd too. He walked right up to us. He was by himself, wearing sunglasses.

"Where is she?" my brother asked.

"Where's the car?" he asked.

"Where's your bag?" I asked.

He raised his arm to show us his roller. His hand was empty. He had sweat rings around his neckline and arm-pits. He was coming down, ready for more.

"Fuck it," he said. "Let's go."

"Where's Mom?" my brother repeated.

"I'll tell you at home," he said. "Just get me out of here."

"No," my brother said.

"Get your fucking ass in the car."

Outside, the sky grown dark, my father kept his sun-glasses on. He unbuttoned his shirt in the Jeep, rolled up his sleeves. He cracked a window, let in the cold. I sat behind him, searched the back of his head for an explanation. For a soft spot in his skull. What excuse would he have this time? What would he accuse her of now? And where was she? How could she not be here? We'd trusted her.

Once inside the apartment he tore through the decorations, marched directly to the phone, ripped the cord from the wall. He threw the answering machine across the room. He drew the blinds, called for a lockdown, radio silence. He collected our keys. He sat us down on the couch, told us that anyone caught contacting our mom would be sent to the brig, guillotined, the biggest fucking *code red* either of us had ever seen.

My brother asked him what happened.

"She thought she was the hero is what happened. She thought she was rescuing you boys from me. This was all my idea. Mine. Mine. It was me. I approached her. I decided to move us back to Kansas. I won back the big account. I invited her out here to help. I'm the savior of this family. I'm the hero in this story."

"Is she OK?" I asked.

"Of course she's fucking OK. I didn't do anything to her. Why are you so fucking concerned about her? Is this a goddamn interrogation? Is that what this is? She's fine. But she won't be bothering us anymore. That's for sure. Who cares anyway? We don't fucking need her. We've never needed her. We can do this without her. We can find a new home. We can start over. In fact this time you boys can pick it. Anywhere in the world. How's that for an idea?" He slapped his knee, laughed aloud. "It's your turn to choose. What do you say? Anywhere in the whole wide world, except back there. You can't go backwards in life. You choose where, anywhere, we can go anywhere, but we're not moving backwards. It's against the laws of nature. Who needs back there anyway? We have each other. We came out here to start over together, didn't we? Family. We're family, remember? Remember?"

My father's eyes suddenly stopped at the fireplace. He saw *The Spirit* missing. The wind rushed out of him. His eyes darted, thinking maybe it had been moved. Something strange happened to me then: I felt myself withdrawing from him. It was as if I had been pulled out of the action of a play. I became the viewer, observing a scene. The soliloquy of a sad and desperate man. I noticed the strain in his face, the hurt, the need for an explanation. My father staggered, pulled himself up straight. He knew the sculpture was gone. And, worse, why. "What do you know about life?" he yelled. "Really, what do you know? You know nothing. You know shit. Tell me one true thing about life. This instant. You can't, can you? Either of you. Tell me one true thing."

We'd gone back into silent mode.

What was there left to say? We'd escaped once already. We'd do it again. We'd call our mom as soon as we could, make sure she was OK, hatch a new plan. Still, I couldn't have been angrier with her. All she had to do was tell us to stay on that bus. We were free. We were out. The fact that she'd put us back inside this apartment was unforgivable. She was gullible and weak, and she couldn't protect us. But we had no other options. Our dad was an act with a single end. His trajectory: down, down, down. He was going to kill himself out here. And it wasn't that I didn't care anymore. He was my father. It was just that we had spent far too long as his audience, right here on this couch. We'd felt happy, hurt, sad here. We'd been reprimanded, confided in. We'd been dazed, embattled, betrayed. We'd slept here, dreamed here, youthful dreams that would never return.

TEN

My father kept all the keys. He canceled the phone
service. He rarely left the house. His new rule was
that one of us had to stay home with him at all times.
Me, mostly. I wasn't allowed out of my room without
permission. We were on winter break. My brother spent
his days at the grocery store. Each shift he'd try our mom
from a pay phone, beg her to call him back. She picked up
once—the first time. "I'm sorry," she told him. "There's
nothing I can do." That was it, all she said. She hung up
immediately and never answered again. She'd chosen to
save herself. It didn't matter. We didn't need her. We were
done relying on anyone but ourselves. My brother lifted
a few dollars from the register whenever he could. My
job was to locate where my father stashed the car keys.
Next payday we were stealing the Jeep, driving straight
to Kansas. We would show up at her door unannounced,
force her to help.

Inside the apartment cracks of daylight plagued my

father. The blinds stayed drawn. The mirror in the living room was covered with a sheet. The folding room screens that once separated my father's office from the living room now blockaded the glass porch door. For a while he'd moved a pizza box from window to window to keep the light out. Finally he just sealed the windows with cardboard and duct tape. Darkness complete, he began obsessing over the ideal placement of objects around the apartment, the folding and refolding of the linens, the washing and rewashing of the dishes, the constant leveling of the New Mexico paintings he'd finally hung, as if he believed he could tinker his way toward perfection. As if he believed he could win us back if he kept the perfect home.

I knew all of this because he sometimes sought me out.

"Son?" He knocked. "Come out here. I want to share something with you."

In the living room my father told me to sit on the couch. He hadn't bathed since Kansas. He hadn't changed his clothes either. His lips were cracked. His fingernails filthy, overgrown. Band-Aids hid the burn blisters on his thumbs. There were sores on his face from picking his skin. He took a seat Indian-style on the floor. I'd never seen my father sit that way. The newfound flexibility of his thinning body jarred me. He emptied a bag of weed onto a plate, sorted out seeds and stems. His hands shook like he had a disease.

"You were my decision," he started. "Did you know that? Your brother was an accident. He wasn't planned like you. To be honest I didn't even want him. I should have guessed how he'd turn out. But as soon as he was born, I knew we needed a second child." He looked up at me. "Do you understand what I'm driving at? You wouldn't exist without me. I thought you up. Trippy, right? Far out. That's what bonds us together. That's the glue, boy. Some cultures might even believe that you owe me your life, wouldn't you say?"

"Yes," I said.

He nodded thoughtfully.

"You know what I was thinking about the other day?" he went on. "That time I took you fishing. I didn't take your brother, did I? Know why? You're special, that's why. Your first cast you dropped the lure right on the fish's head. I knew then, I mean I really knew, like really knew that you had magic in you, son. The same magic I have. You got it from me. It's your birthright. That's another reason our connection is so special. Like when you reeled in that fish. You followed my every instruction, didn't you? It was like you were an extension of me. I mean, that was amazing, right? Like truly amazing, don't you think?"

He glanced at me for affirmation. Weed fell from the rolling paper, missed the plate. He struggled to pick the flecks of pot out of the shags in the carpet. He concentrated deeply, sweeping his tongue again and again across his top lip. He was trying to turn me against my brother. Had his attempts always been this naked? My brother wasn't in the boat that morning because he was sick. The three of us had fled to the Ozarks in the dead of night while my mother slept. They'd been in a fight. My father didn't care that my brother had a fever. He left him in the motel room with a bucket of ice and the TV on. It was more important that she wake up to find us gone.

"What do you think of your brother?" my father asked. He was back to work on the joint. "He's not like us, is he? He doesn't get it like you get it. He's jealous. I've see it in his eyes. He hates you. He even told me that. He knows you're special. There's something special about you, boy. It's a blessing. It's in your DNA. That gene skipped your brother. I'm not trying to be mean. At some point a father has to be honest about his children. What can I do?" He laughed. "One out of two ain't bad."

His mood changed in an instant. His anger suddenly rose. He closed his fist around the failed joint, threw it at me. He shouted for me to go into his bedroom. There was something in his top drawer he wanted me to grab. He said I'd know what I was looking for when I saw it. I jumped up from the couch, followed orders. His outburst had startled me, but once in his room I took the chance to look around for the car keys. First I scanned the top of his dresser. Then I opened each of his drawers as quietly as possible. His clothes were folded, stacked neatly. I checked both top drawers too. One was for socks. The other was full of junk—sunglasses, bristled brushes, a checkbook, an old watch, several blackened spoons, a colorful array of transparent lighters. I saw what he wanted me to grab. From the smell alone I knew the pipe wasn't meant for pot. It was stubby, silver, cylindrical. There was a rubber tube on the mouth piece, and inside the burned bowl was a scorched piece of the copper scouring pads we kept under the sink. I was afraid to touch it, to smell it, cautious of any contact with it at all.

I froze when he called my name. I came running with the pipe.

In the living room he loaded it with pot, took a hit.

"Do you trust me?" he said.

"Of course," I lied.

He took another hit as a demonstration, then passed it to me.

"No, thank you," I said.

His look was so hateful I stopped myself from protesting. My priority was to keep his trust. I grabbed the pipe, took a tiny hit.

"Again," he said. "Just like I showed you."

I took another.

"Bigger," he said.

With the third hit I coughed up smoke. My lungs burned.

"You know, the natives of this land used to share peace pipes with their enemies. It was done to seal alliances. We aren't enemies, though, are we, son? We've always been allies. I've always been your biggest fan, haven't I?" I nodded. "Then tell me what your brother is planning. I know he's up to something. He's always working an angle against me, that little shit. What's up his sleeve? Tell me. Tell me now. What's he got planned?"

"Nothing," I insisted. "He's not planning anything."

"That the truth? Don't lie to me."

"I'm not," I said. "I promise."

Terrible thoughts flooded into my head. I saw my father standing over my brother's body. I imagined bits of flesh stuck in his long savage fingernails. And that grin of his that looked like a snarl. I knew I'd be next, but I wasn't afraid. I felt oddly powerful. My chest expanded. I thought to suck the air right out of my father's lungs from across the room. It was thrilling to picture his breath drawn from him. He wouldn't be able to cry out. He'd be unable to utter a single sound.

"There's an enemy among us," he said. "Whose side are you on?"

"Yours," I lied again.

"You'd tell me if you knew something, wouldn't you?"

"Of course."

"We have to stick together."

"We will."

"Swear."

I swore.

He stood up, came close, kissed my forehead.

"Good boy," he said. "That's all. You're excused."

In my room I paced, feeling the urgency to tell my brother that our dad was out to get him. Then I stared at the wall, replayed the conversation with my father, searched for hidden meanings that might explain how our mother could have just given up on us. I examined my face in the mirror. I was sweating, my heart pounding. My mouth was dry. My wrist itched. With every movement a piece of my clothing seemed to chafe my skin. I stripped down to my underwear. I pulled all the electrical cords from their sockets. I couldn't stand the buzzing. The fearlessness I'd felt only moments before had fled from me. I was petrified, shut in, losing control of my thoughts. There was no way out of myself.

My father's instruction had not helped me reel in the fish that day. After I'd hooked it, the line had gotten wrapped around its body, ripped up its gills. The fish didn't fight at all, just planed across the water's surface. When we got it into the bucket, it flopped around, bleeding. I felt responsible for its suffering and obligated to watch it die. My father thought I was being morose. He moved the bucket away from me, placed a rag over the top. I cast my line once more, and—even now as I waited out this nightmare hunkered down in the corner of my room—I got lost in the beauty of that day. The sun was bright. The water at the surface of the lake was molten. The first patches of fall had blossomed in the tree line. Small waves from a soft breeze swayed the boat gently. Enormous rocks slept beneath us like dormant elephants. And then the fish would tail-slap the bucket again.

I watched my father cross the street to the pay phone. I'd peeled back a corner of the cardboard he'd used to seal my window. I'd been studying his habit from here. Every few days he'd make a call from the corner. Then he'd come back home to wait. A half hour later a white Civic with tinted windows would honk outside the apartment. My father wouldn't even let his dealer inside anymore. He'd go out to the parking lot to meet him.

When he was out of sight, I darted to his room, searched beneath the bed, under the mattress, between the pillows. I threw open the drawer to his nightstand. I tried the little table that shelved his television and VCR. I patted down his clothes hanging in the closet. I even checked his shoes. I scanned his bathroom, opened the medicine cabinet, looked beneath the sink. Short on time I ran to the peephole in the front door. My father wasn't back yet. I racked my brain for where to check next. I tried his office. I opened up the desk drawers, lifted the files out of the filing cabinet. I even sifted through paperclips and emptied the cup in which he kept pens. The keys were nowhere to be found. I was cutting it close. I'd have a few more minutes when he stepped out to the Civic. I hurried to my room, closed the door.

He walked back into the apartment seconds later.

An eye on the street, I waited for the Civic to arrive, my thoughts scrambling. My dad wasn't as predictable as I'd assumed. I needed to put myself inside his head, think like he thought. I needed to make a decision. I desperately reviewed the places I'd already checked, unsure where else to look. I settled on his dresser. I'd been jumpy a few days ago when he sent me in for the pipe. Maybe I'd missed something. Maybe he was arrogant enough to have already pointed me in the right direction.

The Civic pulled up, honked. My father walked out the front door. I shot to his room. I went straight for the pipe drawer, sorted through his paraphernalia. The keys weren't there. I lifted up the stacks of folded clothes from his bottom drawers. There was nothing beneath them. I opened his sock drawer last. In my eagerness, though,

I yanked the entire thing out of the track. Socks went tumbling all over the floor. I rushed to collect them. I had only a few more pairs to grab when I felt something solid hidden in a single black dress sock. I reached in, pulled out the key ring plus a wad of bills. I'd found his money stash. From a quick count the total was maybe five thousand dollars. Fury consumed me: How long had we been scraping by? How guilty had we felt over any expense? We didn't even dare ask for the things we needed. And how many months had my brother been working at the grocery store, making sure we were both OK?

But I was also dancing inside. We were going home.

I heard the front door open.

I was caught. There was no escaping his room in time. I started to panic. I couldn't risk blowing the whole operation right now. I had just found the keys. There'd be another chance to grab them in a few days. I'd be quicker then, in and out. It would be safer too. I stuffed the key ring and the cash back into the black dress sock, grabbed the last few pairs left on the floor, tossed all of it into the drawer. I jumped up. The drawer slipped easily back into the track. I was still facing the dresser when I heard my father stop dead in his doorway.

"What are you doing?" he said. "Why are you out of your room?"

I thought of only one thing to do. I opened his top

drawer, pulled out the pipe, brought it to him. "I'm an extension of you," I said. "Right?"

His anger fell away, but his suspicion was still strong.

"Like with the fish, remember?" I asked him. "That's what you said."

His eyes swelled with love.

"You're a good boy," he said. "You're my only good boy."

My father put a rock in the pipe, smoked right in front of me. I watched him come to life in the living room. His muscles tensed, eyes dilated and darting. He raved about the injustices he'd suffered throughout his life. "Did you know that I was fired the year you were born? Two babies and a wife. The Amalekite sure as hell wasn't working." He jumped topics. "My mom died so young. And my father preferred my brother. Your brother is actually a lot like mine. My brother stole my father from me the same way yours is trying to steal you." Then, breaking down, he said, "I'm being ripped apart at the seams, son. There's a monster inside me trying to get out. I never wanted kids. I'm not built for them. I never wanted them."

When my brother got home, I told him all that had happened. The places I'd searched, how close I'd been to getting caught, how I'd found the car keys in the sock drawer. I told him that I watched our dad smoke crack. I emphasized his paranoia. And I warned my brother again about our father's vendetta against him. My brother was distracted, withdrawn. He seemed to be communing with some private fear. I'd saved the money stash for last. When I told him, his eyes lit up. They finally focused on me. "Holy fuck!" he said. "You're fucking kidding me. Holy Fuck!" Then he told me he'd been caught lifting cash from the register today. He'd run from the premises, penniless, the paycheck we needed to get away gone.

There was a knock at our apartment the following morning. I peeled back the cardboard, peeked out the corner of our window. A cop car was in the parking lot. My brother tried hard to keep his cool. I told him to stay put. I got up, opened our bedroom door. My father was looking through the peephole. He turned to me, unfazed. I'd expected him to be terrified. He raised his finger slowly to his lips, turned back to the door. The cops knocked, announced themselves. They knocked again. And then a fourth time. My father kept his composure, waited them out. When the cops left, he didn't address me. He didn't even look in my direction. He didn't seem to care what they were here for. He shuffled away from the door—the picture of calm.

The cops returned every day after. My father grew more and more agitated. He refused to leave his bedroom except to check the peephole whenever they knocked. He'd then hurry back to his room. To keep his suspicion low we decided that my brother should pretend to still be going to work. He went out early in the morning to avoid the cops, came home late at night. He waited in the park all day for me to come running with the cash and keys. My father hadn't called his dealer since the last time, so I hadn't had an opportunity to retrieve them. At dark my brother took risks to keep us fed. He looted the expired food from the grocery store Dumpster. He also kept me up late these nights to go over the plan, always asking questions. "What if he catches you going through his drawer? What do you do then?" I had to be ready for anything, he said. I had to be prepared. He told me not to act out of desperation. He made me promise. He even folded back the cardboard from our window, unlocked the sash. "This is your escape route if there's trouble," he said. "If you have to run, meet me in the park." I knew he felt terrible that our freedom now relied solely on me. He wouldn't forgive himself if something bad happened. It's why he insisted we go over and over the details.

We never guessed, though, that our dad would make me page his dealer for him.

My father was vile that day, crashing hard. I pleaded with him.

"I don't feel safe," I said. "Please don't make me go."

He grabbed me by the arm, dragged me to the front door, threw me out.

As I walked across the street I kept my eye out for my brother. Even though the park was on the other side of the building, he was supposed to have situated himself somewhere he could look onto both the phone booth and the back porch. I didn't see him, but I hoped he saw me. At the pay phone I did as instructed. I dialed the number my father had written on a piece of paper, typed in his special code, made sure to hit pound before hanging up. I hurried home knowing I'd sneak into my dad's room the second he went out to the Civic.

Back inside the apartment my father asked me if I'd used his special code.

"Yes," I said.

"You make sure . . . " he started.

"I hit the pound button," I interrupted him.

He glared at me. I kept my eyes away from his.

"You make sure to hit the pound button?" he finished his question.

"Yes," I said.

He nodded. "Go to your room."

A half hour later he was in my room, agitated. "Where the fuck is he?"

"I swear," I said. "I hit the pound button."

"And the code?"

"And the code."

He was adamant that I'd made a mistake. He told me to go make the page again.

"Why don't we wait another fifteen minutes?" I suggested.

I barely got the sentence out. I came to on the floor, blackness receding, the right side of my face turning hot. My father was standing over me. I rolled onto my knees until the dizziness passed. Then, a hand on the wall, I made my way to the front door.

I went across the street, paged the guy again.

On my way back through the parking lot, my brother still not in sight, the white Civic drove past me. I hustled to the apartment. I tried the door. The knob stuck. I knocked. My father opened it to a crack.

"Your guy is here," I told him. The Civic honked. "See?"

He slammed the door on me, flicked the dead bolt.

I knew then that he was going to make me do the deal for him too. I blamed myself for not being prepared. What else did I have to do in my room these days but to work through all the possibilities? This was it. This was supposed to be the moment I would get us free. *Get us free*—my father's phrase. I was revolted to realize that he was so much a part of me. I wanted to expel him from my being. I wanted him out, exorcised. When he opened the door again, the chain lock was latched. "I hate you," I said. "You don't give a shit about us. Let me back inside." He slipped a wad of cash through the crack. "Fuck that," I said. "No way."

"No way?" he said. "Make me come out there, I'll show you no way."

The car honked again.

My brother and I would take him by surprise tonight. We'd bang down our dad's bedroom door with bats. I turned giddy over it. At least I wouldn't flee this place without leaving my mark on him. What was he going to do? Call the cops? But I couldn't say no to him right now. My father was nastier than ever. I didn't want to meet his rage alone. I needed him distracted until my brother got home.

The Civic honked a third time. The driver held the horn.

"Get moving," he said.

I ripped the money from his hand. He shut the door.

It took all my anger to muster the nerve to walk out to the parking lot and up to the Civic. But once there I just stood, unsure what to do next. The window finally rolled down. A blond man in the driver seat had bad acne scars, pores like pits. A woman sat shotgun. I avoided eye contact with both of them.

"Here," I said. I showed him the cash.

He started to roll up his window.

"You don't understand," I said. "I can't go back in there without it."

The window stopped. He must have heard my desperation. Or she had.

"I don't fuck with kids," he said. But he told me to get in anyway.

I climbed into the backseat, handed him the money. He counted it.

"He's only got to page me once," the driver said.

"I'm sorry," I said.

"Motherfucker makes me honk three times . . . Sends out a kid."

I told him I was sorry again.

"Hundred," he said to the woman.

She handed me a mini Ziploc. My palms were sweaty, and I wished I'd wiped them on the seat before making the exchange. Then I wasn't sure whether to look at the bag or not. I was also uncertain whether I was now excused. She must have sensed my hesitation because she asked me if I was scared.

"Yes, ma'am."

"You go to school?"

"Yes, ma'am."

"That mark on your face—that from your dad?"

I nodded.

"Get out." The driver raised his voice. "Get the fuck out of my car." He slipped the Civic into reverse. I jumped out quickly. But soon the car stopped. He rolled his window down again, called me over. "Tell your dad if he ever pulls this shit again." I nodded. He took a long look at me, shook his head, pointed to his upper chest. "This is where a punch starts from," he said. "See it coming next time."

He drove off.

My father let me back into the apartment only after I assured him that I'd done what he'd asked. Inside, I handed over the mini Ziploc. I started to my room.

"Stop," he said. He examined the bag. "Where's the rest?"

"That's what he gave me."

"I gave you two hundred dollars."

"You gave me one hundred."

"Bullshit," he said. "Where's the other bag?"

"That's all he gave me," I repeated.

"Your jacket—hand it over."

I tossed him my jacket. He searched through it.

"Turn out your pockets," he said.

I emptied my pockets.

He got in my face, forced my T-shirt off me. He threw it against the wall.

"Shoes and socks."

I took a step back, removed my shoes and socks. He tossed them aside too.

"Take off your pants," he said. "Now!"

I wasn't wearing any underwear, I confessed.

He grimaced. "Why not?"

"I need to do laundry."

"You've always been a filthy fucking child," he said. "You disgust me. I'm going to vomit, you repulse me so much. Take off your pants, you disgusting piece of shit."

"I swear I'm not hiding anything from you. All you gave me was a hundred."

I saw the slap coming, ducked it. We both stood there surprised. Then my father faked his right, punched me in the eye with his left. I welled up with tears. A self-satisfied grin stretched my father's face. "Take off your pants," he said again.

I took off my jeans, tossed them to him.

He checked the pockets, turned them upside down, shook them out. He stood thinking for a moment, engaged in inner counsel. His eyes suddenly fell hard on me.

He told me to turn around, bend over.

"Dad," I said. "Please."

He stripped off his belt.

"All right," I told him. "But when would I have had time to do anything like this?"

The belt cracked me in the face. I lost hearing on my right side. The taste of blood followed quickly. I'd thought at first I was bleeding from the ear, but I felt my lip begin to swell. "Shut up," he said. "Turn around."

I turned around.

"Bend over."

I bent over.

"Cough."

I coughed.

The belt cut across my butt. I did my best to keep from whimpering.

"Where's the other bag?" he said.

"There wasn't one."

This time he lashed me across the back.

"Then where's my money?"

"It's all you gave me."

He struck me on the back a second time. And then a third.

"How long have you been on your brother's side?"

"What? No," I said. "I'm not."

"Don't fucking lie to me. Tell me the truth."

I professed my innocence.

"Liar!" he screamed. And he let me have it. He whipped me again and again, all over, not caring where the belt found flesh, yelling the entire time, "After all I've done for you. I gave up my life to protect you. I saved you from your mother. I should have drowned you both at birth. I should have smothered you with a fucking pillow. This is how you repay me? Where's the other bag, you ungrateful shit? Where's my fucking money? Give me what's mine."

He could rip me apart with that belt strap, mark up

my body. He could turn me around and do the front side next. I wasn't going to protect myself, or even cry out. I wouldn't give him the satisfaction. In my mind I banished him to his worst version of hell. We never loved you. My mother never loved you. You're going to be alone the rest of your life. I fanned the flames of his paranoia. I've been plotting against you since we moved here. You're going to jail. Your dealer's never selling to you again either. You better conserve that precious bag of yours. With every crack of the belt I taunted him. Whip me all you like, whip me until you're gassed. Until you suck wind. And when his arm was too heavy to raise again, when he was weak, worn out, ready to quit, that's when I planned to strike. That's when I'd rise up full of vengeance, cut the bastard down.

I woke in the night. I had no idea how I'd gotten to bed. I tried my brother's name aloud. My mouth too dry, I worked up some saliva and tried again. His name rang out clearly this time. Nothing came back out of the darkness. It hurt everywhere to roll over. My back seized. My body braced. I winced, and my face hurt. When the spasm subsided, I sat up slowly. My right eye had swollen shut. My left adjusted. Our bedroom took form. I was alone. I stood, walked over to my brother's side of the room. My head throbbed in pure pronounced seconds. My heart sank as I felt his cold sheets. I climbed into his bed, pulled the covers to my chin. A tear rolled down my cheek. I lay there still as possible, breathing gently, knowing that I could endure the pain if I managed not to move.

I slept. Each time I woke, I was torn between worlds, always willing to leave whatever dream I was in, but never ready to fully awaken. The last dream: my father brought me to a long candlelit hallway. The candles were posted at even intervals along a checkered marble floor and the wooden barrel-vaulted ceiling shined dimly overhead like the hull of a massive overturned ship. Until my dad pointed out the wall, I hadn't realized that the paint was cracking, flaking off. My job was to touch it up, he explained, but I wasn't supposed to paint over every crack. I was only to paint where the candles threw light onto the wall. I went to work, taking great pleasure brightening these little spots, filling in the glow, deciding for myself where the candlelight ended and darkness began. I worked through the night. But as morning came, daylight began to creep down the hallway, and all these imperfect circles started popping up along the wall, and to my horror the cracks now seemed to emanate from them like high-voltage currents.

Then I was awake for good. I could tell by the direct light on the cardboard that it was morning. My mind wouldn't let me sleep. I lay there one minute at a time for what seemed like hours. My brother still wasn't home. I worried about him. I brimmed with a strange kind of sadness. As if I were full of emptiness. As if emptiness were an abundant thing. Maybe this feeling was the reason my mother couldn't get out of bed for months after their separation. And where was she? I needed her now. An angry voice inside told me to stop being dramatic, suck it up. She had abandoned us. The escape plan had failed. I'd let my brother down. Now he was missing. I shouldn't act so surprised—these were my circumstances. This was my life. And outside the door my father lurked. I hated the idea that maybe he'd helped me to bed last night. I didn't want his kindness. His cruelty was less confusing. I made my way to the bathroom to take a look.

I was struck first to find myself naked. I'd forgotten I wasn't wearing any clothes. I saw my face in the mirror. On the left side a burn from the belt spread across my cheek, all the way to my mouth, where a tooth had punctured my lip. On the right my eye was a slit from the swelling, sensitive to light. I thought back to when he punched me. How pleased he'd been with his cleverness. When I found my face in the mirror again, I felt gutless. I was scared to turn around. The skin on my back was tight, tender. The muscles were traumatized, going in and out of spasms. It took work to stand still, upright, balanced. Finally I just did it, turned around and looked over my shoulder into the mirror. Across most of my back red and purple welts overlay a dark pool of swirling colors, like something wicked had used my body to make a finger painting. I looked away, faced the wall, tried to fight a surge inside me. But anger rose so sharply that I started to tear up. From there I lost myself entirely. Cries I didn't recognize as my own came out of me. Sounds I never knew humans could make. Sobs shook my body from somewhere deep. Snot and tears ran into my mouth. I wept, and I moaned, and after, exhaustion settled over me, and I barely managed to put on pajamas before making my way back to my brother's bed to sleep.

I woke in the afternoon to a knock at the front door. The police car was back in the parking lot. Outside my room I heard my father's footsteps. The cops knocked again. Then one started to speak. I went to my door to listen. He asked my father to open up. It was about my brother. They'd picked him up in the park yesterday. He'd spent the night in a detention center, holding out, refusing to say who he was. Today he'd finally relented. They'd tried calling but the phone was shut off. "Please open the door, sir," the cop said. "It's important we speak to you. We know you're home. We know that's your Jeep in the parking lot. Open up, please," he said. "Open the door. Sir, open up. It's about your son."

They knocked and knocked. He didn't answer.

I cracked my door. My father was standing at the peep-hole. He signaled me to come take a look. As I walked over, I felt the need to hide my face, to apologize for my appearance. I was afraid to remind him of last night. He stepped back, pointed me to the peephole. I peered out. Two police officers stood before the door. A third man, in plainclothes, had positioned himself behind the cops. My brother was next to him, head down. The man in plainclothes stepped forward, introduced himself. He said he was a case manager. He explained that my brother had been caught stealing from the grocery store earlier this week, that he'd run, and that the cops had been looking for him for several days now. The store was willing to drop the charges, the case manager emphasized, but a conversation needed to be had first. "Sir," he said, gesturing to my brother. "You don't want your son sleeping in a detention center again, right? Please open the door. Like I said, we just need to have a conversation with you."

My father put his hands on my shoulders, squeezed. I hardly felt the pain. I shuddered instead from the thrill of hatred I felt for him. He spoke quietly into my ear: "See? I told you your brother was against us. Didn't I tell you? Now you believe me? He's the enemy. He's a traitor. He dug his own grave. I'm sure as hell not jumping in to save him. Are you? Huh? Are you?"

"No," I lied, my tone hushed like his.

"Good boy." Then he whispered, "You know I forgive you for last night, right?"

"I know."

"I always forgive you, don't I?"

I nodded.

"Be my eyes?" he asked.

"Of course."

"Let me know when they're gone."

I said OK.

My father turned, started back to his bedroom.

I kept my eye on my brother. When he finally looked up, his face was remade with a strange combination of sadness and certainty. As if he knew about the beating I'd taken last night. As if he knew we were never going home. I longed to comfort him, to tell him that none of this was his fault, for him to sense that it was me at the peephole. I ached to lock eyes, to see him smile again. Like years ago, lying on the beast's stomach in the living room of the old house. My father is defeated, tackled into submission. He puffs his stomach out, plays dead. Our heads rise with his belly. Our necks crane. Light from the window paints my brother's cheek. A beautiful smile breaks over his face. Mine too. I imagined us returning to that moment, back before our dad releases all his air in a single sudden shot, back when our minds are still, and we have no notion that the bottom is about to drop from beneath us.

ONE OF THE BOYS

My heart was beating so fast I thought it might quit. My hands were going numb from nerves. My muscles felt like they were slowing down, selling me out. I reached up, unlatched the chain lock, flicked the dead bolt, opened the door. My eyes filled with water, and light rushed in.

EPILOGUE

EPILOGUE

We pull out of his driveway around noon. My father will do the sixteen hours straight. My brother is in the backseat. I've been selected navigator, the directions simple. A few hours on I-35S will lead us out of Kansas, away from our mother—*the war* now over. Heading south, my only responsibility is to remind my father to make a *Ralph* when we hit Oklahoma City. That's it. The only turn. I-40W is a straight shot through the rest of Oklahoma, the Texas Panhandle, into New Mexico, all the way to our new life in Albuquerque. I leave the road atlas open on my lap anyway. My father occasionally checks in with me.

"What's next?" he asks.

"Hang a Ralph at OKC," I say.

"That it?"

"That's it."

He tousles my hair. He gets a kick out of this kind of back-and-forth.

"How far to the state line?" my brother asks.

I size my thumb to the mileage scale on the legend.

My father tosses me a toothpick. "Here, use this."

I size it to the scale.

"You know, back in the old days," he starts as though narrating a documentary, "say you wanted to make a table that was the perfect size for your family, well, instead of using fancy measurement tools, people used to mark a stick. Think about it. You don't need numbers to figure out how high you want your table to be, now do you? Then they'd use the stick to measure the lumber. Simplifies it all, takes the math out of it. They called them story sticks," he says with a funny country drawl. "Wait." My father stops me. "Let's see how accurate you are."

He resets the odometer. The zeros roll forward.

"Drum roll," my brother says.

I take my time measuring, build the tension.

"The distance to Oklahoma is . . . " I pause. "Four and a half toothpicks."

"In miles," my father says.

"Story stick, Dad. Takes the math out of it."

"Glad you're making yourself useful, son."

We all laugh.

My father makes a show of looking around him, into the mirrors, out the windows. My brother and I follow him, try to figure out what has suddenly caught his attention. To the horizon the wheat fields are lush. The stalks, tall as children, bow in the direction of the wind. It's summer, the sun high. But for a low cloud and its shadow in the field, the sky and earth are pale and wide.

"Are we still in fucking Kansas?" my father says.

He bottoms out the pedal.

Before long we pass the no-man's-mile between a sign that tells us we are leaving Kansas and one that welcomes us to Oklahoma. I watch my dad from the corner of my eye as we cross the state line. He leans his head back into the headrest. He places his forearm on the window frame. The wind flaps his shirt collar, combs through his hair. He's calm. Behind his sunglasses, I imagine, my father's eyes are closed.

We make a pit stop in a small town. My father tells us to pump, he'll pay. When the tank is full, my brother parks the Jeep in front of the entrance to the station. My father comes out a moment later, dangles a bathroom key at us, disappears around the corner.

He's gone awhile before one of us goes to check on him.

I knock on the door, call his name. He's fine, he says.

I return to the Jeep, reclaim shotgun.

"Well?" my brother asks.

I shrug.

Looking at the entrance to the gas station I realize a change in our position. My brother has moved the Jeep over a few spots. We are suddenly in a separate reality, nearly identical to this one, except all that's different is where we park here today. As if my brother has been given the choice to change one thing in the whole of time, and this is it.

"You moved the Jeep?"

"You noticed."

My father turns the corner, slips into the station to return the key.

"You think he will?" my brother asks.

A moment later my father comes out, takes over my seat.

He informs my brother that it's time for him to learn how to drive on a highway.

"You sure?" my brother wants to know.

"Are you?" my father responds.

After an hour on the road my father tells my brother to merge onto I-235S for Oklahoma City. From the interstate he points out a gap in the skyline. We all look to the city, transfixed, our heads gradually turning to keep our eyes pointed downtown. There are several yellow tower cranes and hoist elevators poking out from between the buildings. He has my brother pull off the highway, drive a half mile. Soon, on the passenger side, we approach a fenced-in lot where three months ago, our dad reminds us, a Ryder truck filled with ammonium nitrate fertilizer sheared the facade of the Alfred P. Murrah building. Posted on the fence that surrounds the site are notes, photos, signs, real flowers, fake flowers, toys, American flags, teddy bears. We square the block. My brother drives slowly. As I listen to my father, I imagine a hundred and sixty-eight corpses being fished out of the rubble. Where once stood the Federal Building, there is now a vacant lot—a prison yard, my dad thinks, for an angry mob of souls.

"Can you feel it?" he asks us. "Can you?"

"Feel what?" my brother says.

"I'm not sure I've ever been this close to evil."

We make our way back to the interstate, take the *Ralph* onto I-40W. The rest of Oklahoma seems ominous. We pass oil fields, see pump jacks nodding like horse heads. At one point we come upon a stretch of white hundred-foot wind turbines, their blades turning with the patience of a rock. If not for their sleek geometry I might have thought they were prehistoric, that the wind generated from their rotations, and not the other way around.

We make a big deal about it when we pass from Oklahoma into Texas. We are getting closer. We can feel it. My brother drives us into the sunset, racing the day to the horizon, stretching time. We'll even gain an hour once we hit New Mexico.

*　　*　　*

It's past dark when we pull into a diner in Amarillo. My father wants coffee and pie. Inside, he walks straight up to a waitress. Slender, athletic, with plastic-looking legs, she points him to the bathroom. He starts away from her, turns back, says something. We can tell by her smile that she's taken with him.

"What's that?" he asks when he arrives at the table.

She is setting down our order. "Coffee and pie on three," she says.

"That better be decaf," he tells us.

We snicker behind the heavy mugs, pleased with ourselves for having gotten something past him. He winks at us.

"Is this heaven?" he asks the waitress, putting his hands behind his head.

"I ain't that pretty," she says.

He stays a step ahead of her. "I was referring to the enormous Cross we passed a few miles back. Must've been two hundred feet tall."

"Quite a sight," she says. "Where y'all coming from?"

"Where're we going to is a better question."

She looks at me and my brother as if to play hard to get. "Well?" she asks.

"New Mexico," I say.

"Albuquerque," my brother says.

162

"You running from the law? Y'all look like a gang of desperados."

"It's not the law we're running from," my father says.

He gives a sad half smile, shows her his bare ring finger.

She looks over at us kids again. We keep our heads down, embarrassed by his honesty but also playing up the story. She turns back to my father, holds him in her gaze. He looks at her. We do too, all of us disarmed. Her green eyes are edged with a hazy blue border, and her hair, dirty blond, is pulled up in a too-tight ponytail. The two of them exchange sweet smiles. They are locked in.

She reaches for my father's hand, puts two fingers on his wrist. She keeps her eyes on the wall clock. Under the table my brother taps my knee. I lean into his shoulder. From the caffeine my fingertips tingle, palms sweat, heart races. Watching her take my father's pulse is thrilling.

A half minute later she says, "This one might be in heaven."

"Nothing there?" my brother says.

"No heartbeat?" I ask.

"More like a hammer," she says.

My father slaps the table with approval.

"Shame y'all won't be staying long in Amarillo." She pouts, walks away.

Back on the road my father drives. My brother is in the front seat. I sit behind him. We pass around the restaurant bill on which the waitress wrote her name, her number. "Luck comes in streaks," my father says. He lets the piece of paper fly out the window. We share his confidence as we cross into New Mexico. We relax into our seats, feel the triumph of the day. It's the dead of night. The moon has risen. Too soon, though, the coffee wears off. My eyelids grow heavy. I want to stay awake for Albuquerque. I want to complete the drive as a team, as one of the boys. I crack my window to keep sleep at bay. But it's hopeless. I soon find myself staring past the stars into the darkest night, sinking into the sky, knowing that in my first unthinking moment, tomorrow will have already begun.

I wake to the smell of cigar smoke. I am sprawled out on the backseat. I sit up. We're pulled over on the shoulder of the road. The first light of day is behind us.

"Where are we?" I ask.

"Just east of Albuquerque," my father says.

"How long have we been sitting here?"

"Little while."

My brother wakes up. "Why aren't we moving?" he asks.

"This is how I want us to see our new home for the first time," my father says. "Roll your windows down."

We do.

"Listen."

ONE OF THE BOYS

I hear nothing. Not the low hum of power lines, not the whoosh of tires, not the chirp of birds, not a train whistle blow and stop, blow and stop. Just off the road shadows begin to appear. Night recedes. From out of the darkness there is dirt, bramble, distance. The air is dry. How different this place is from Kansas—that's my father's point. The seasons in New Mexico are not as pronounced. The temperature gets a little cooler or hotter as the year goes on, daylight lasts a little longer or shorter, there's less vegetation—fewer signs. Life in the desert is found in the testimony of small changes. It is nearly a secret.

"You boys ready?" he asks.

"Yes," I say.

"Hell yes," my brother says.

My father starts the Jeep, slips into first, veers onto the road. He shifts a gear. The engine revs. "Giddyup," he shouts. He punches the clutch, bottoms out the pedal. We get going, gain speed. My brother and I stick our heads out the window, gaze forward, take in the air, the change, the wind. We are birds in low flight. We are kids again, the three of us, just like he'd promised. My father points ahead. "Look." To the west the land swells along the horizon. My father lets out a battle cry. My brother and I whoop like Indians. Mountains emerge, red as stirred embers.

ACKNOWLEDGMENTS

For his assuring presence, advocacy, and enthusiasm, I am indebted to my agent, Bill Clegg. For the light their brilliance has shined on these pages, I am grateful to my editors at Scribner, Nan Graham and Daniel Loedel. I am likewise indebted to Bella Lacey at Granta for her superb dusting of my prose. I will forever count myself fortunate to have studied with the ever-generous teachers at Syracuse University, namely Dana Spiotta, Arthur Flowers, Mary Karr, and George Saunders. A thank-you is also in order to my workshop—Alex, Annie, Caitlin, Jessie, and Oscar—and to the many other students at SU next to whom I had the privilege of learning.

To Jude, thank you for being such a razor-sharp reader.

To Rivka, thank you for your support, kindness, and wisdom through the years.

To George, thank you for helping me realize the

ACKNOWLEDGMENTS

ambition to be my best self. Oh, yes, thanks for the ice skates, too.

Most importantly, to Justine, my first reader and my last, thank you for being such an inexhaustible champion of this book (and of me). Everything I've ever written I've left unfinished, but for: I love you.